George Essex Evans

The Repentance of Magdalene Despar and Other Poems

George Essex Evans

**The Repentance of Magdalene Despar and Other Poems**

ISBN/EAN: 9783744764278

Printed in Europe, USA, Canada, Australia, Japan

Cover: Foto ©Andreas Hilbeck / pixelio.de

More available books at **www.hansebooks.com**

OF

# MAGDALENÈ DESPAR

## *AND OTHER POEMS.*

BY

## G. ESSEX EVANS.

𝔏𝔬𝔫𝔡𝔬𝔫:

SAMPSON LOW, MARSTON, SEARLE, & RIVINGTON,

LIMITED

ST. DUNSTAN'S HOUSE, FETTER LANE, FLEET STREET.

1891.

# DEDICATION.

## In Memoriam: M. A. E.

*January*, 22, 1890.

### I.

Beyond the deepening shadows of Death's night
    God giveth perfect light ;
When earthly love and light no more can shine
    He giveth love divine ;
And on the weary heart, where sorrows cease,
    He sets His seal of Peace.

### II.

His Rest is sure, His Love is strong and deep.
    Why should we weep
For those who, in the silence gently stirred,
    His Angel's voice have heard,
And following, passed, led by a tender hand
    Into the Unknown Land ?

# CONTENTS.

———◦◇◦———

6 *CONTENTS.*

# THE REPENTANCE OF MAGDALENÈ DESPAR.

## PART I.

### I.

" O THE richness of Morn ! O the freshness of
Spring !
When the heart is upborne as a bird on the wing ;
When the fire in the hearts of the poets bursts forth in
the songs that they sing ;

" In the depths of my heart when my girlhood was
young
I have felt myself part of the songs that they sung,
Of words that were mingled with music in measures that
trembled and swung ;

" When I dreamt that the world was made only
for me—
The white waves that curled on the shores of the
sea—
The myst'ry of Nature—the breath of the Spirit that
broods over forest and lea.

" In the midst of the wild as a wild-flower I grew
With the heart of a child that was tender and true
In the calm of seclusion unbroken where pleasures were
simple and few.

"I can see my home still, the wide view it com-
mands
From the crest of the hill where the head-station
stands
O'erlooking the waste of blue waters that circle the shimmering sands.

"In the bright bygone hours never shadowed by
care,
In a garden of flowers where the roses were fair,
They held me the Queen of the Roses—the purest and
stateliest there.

"Not till then had I known that I wore on my
face
As a light that is thrown from a heavenly place
The jewel of beauty, impearled on my brow, the sign-
manual of fairness and grace.

"Tho' I knew not of love, of the radiance that
gleams
As a light from above, as the glint of bright beams
That colour the grayness of Life with the richness and
beauty of dreams ;

"Yet I formed an ideal of the fancies that start,
Of whispers that steal from the depths of the heart,
And I mused o'er a love that was deathless, that sorrow
and pain could not part."

II.

"In the youth of the year
When Winter is dead and the strength of her reign has
. been broken,
When Nature has donned the soft colours of Spring as a
token,
And hearts that were weary are filled with a gladness
unspoken
That Spring-time is here ;

"When on forest and plain
Rich hues lie unsullied, reborn in their brightness and
splendour,
In dark-green and emerald, carmine and azure, tints
subtle and tender,
Fresh from the hand of the Artist Immortal, the touch
of the Sender                            .
Who paints them again ;

" When solitudes teem
With the life and the glory with which all existence is
glowing,
When laden with music and rich with perfume the slow
zephyrs are blowing,
When Spring waxing strong with the strength of young
days into Summer is growing,
I woke from my dream.

" And, waking, I passed
From the dreaming of visions whose influence held me
and bound me
To the light of a faith and the strength of a love that will
ever be round me,
For here, on the desolate station, the Fate that I dreamt
of had found me—
Had found me at last !

"Not the hero and lord
Of the castles I built in the hours of an indolent leisure,
Not the youth in the flush of his prime seeking beauty
    and pleasure,
Whose heart was afire with high hope and a love without
    measure
        For her he adored.

"Not such was the man
To whom I had given the best gift that a woman possesses,
The faith of a heart yet untouched when her soft voice
    confesses
The passionate sweetness of Love with its sighs and
    caresses—
        Giving all that she can.

"The autumn of life
Had silvered the locks once as dark as the wing of the
    raven,
Had tempered the passions that oft make a strong spirit
    craven,
And Time's rugged ploughshare on face and on brow had
    engraven
        The scars of the strife.

"In his eyes Love still sees
That light that in sorrow or trouble burns brighter and
    clearer
From the soul of a strong man and just, to whom honour
    is dearer
Than wealth or high fame or soft ties that are firmer and
    nearer
        And better than these.

" Why need be retold
What is old as the Earth is, but still in its passion and
  yearning
Is new, ever new, with its longings, hopes, fears, and
  heart-burning,
Is new, ever new, to the heart that its soft creed is
  learning—
      The new tale that is old ?


      " O light was my heart
When the bells from the church on my marriage morn
  gaily were pealing,
And we on the steps of God's altar together were kneeling
And uttered our vows before Him who our compact was
  sealing
      Till Death did us part.

      .      .      .      .      .      .

      " Ah ! Why had they said
Not age with gray hairs and grave face for bright youth
  was created,
Only Youth in the glow of Life's morning with Youth
  should be mated ?
Ah ! Why do those words haunt me now in these days
  evil-fated
      When I would I were dead ? "


### III.

" Life is like a mighty river rolling onward to the sea,
Past low meadows, rocky headlands, still it flows un-
  ceasingly,
Swerves in curves, and flows in stretches, ever varying its
  force
As the banks contract or broaden in the channels of its
  course.

But to all who sail its waters comes a time when Fate
may glide
Slowly, calmly, gently onwards with the ripples of its tide ;
So to me ere yet I dreamt of aught of sorrow, shame, or ill,
Came a time of sweet contentment when my days were
pure and still.

" Four long years we lived together on the station by the
sea,
Far from that old well-loved homestead which had been
the world to me ;
Here no belts of yellow sandbanks form a stretch of
shimm'ring strand,
But the beetling crags and headlands rise abrupt on either
hand ;
And for gentle ripples falling with slow music on the
shore,
Wild and high above the storm wind you may hear the
breakers roar.
Four long years in cloud and sunshine lived we on this
rugged coast,
Where the cries of wand'ring sea-birds seem the wailings
of a ghost ;
Where on winter eves at midnight bursts the giant hurricane,
Shakes the four walls of the station till the timbers start
again.

.    .    .    .    .    .

" Four long years in cloud and sunshine lived we by the
restless sea,
Where each day was as another in its calm monotony ;
But my heart was changing slowly, and I felt with secret
pain
Friendship take the place of Love where only Love itself
should reign.

Was it only woman's fancy made me think him cold,
   austere—
Till I felt the love I bore him tempered with an unknown
   fear ?
Was it that my heart rebellious scorned that grave and
   courteous air,
Longing for a wilder spirit with more fire to do and dare?
Wrapt in cares of which he spoke not, tho' his smile was
   kind and mild—
I, a wife, with woman's longings, to be treated as a child !
So I nursed my wrongs in silence, musing o'er my wounded
   pride,
Till a barrier grew between us whom no barrier should
   divide.
Often in those days I fancied I could hear those words of
   truth—
' Youth, not age with fifty winters, should be wedded unto
   youth.'

" Three long years in cloud and sunshine we had watched
   our darling grow
Like a flower upon the mountain, bright as light, and pure
   as snow ;
Only one was mine to cherish, but a fairy full of grace,
In whose laughing eyes and features once again I saw my
   face ;
All the love and all the yearning in a heart as wild as mine,
All my hopes and my ambition centred in this gift divine.
Where to southward of the station lies a little sanded bay,
Bringing back to me the memory of a careless childhood's
   day,
Here at times I oft would linger with the child in early
   spring,
Dreaming of the Unknown Future, wond'ring what the
   years would bring.

"Was it that a curse from Heaven lingered over mine
and me?
Oft methought I heard God's anger in the moaning of
the sea;
For the child I loved so dearly, the sole solace of my
pride,
Like a flower before the storm blast sickened in the Spring
and died.
And we laid her in her beauty on the cliffs beside the bay,
Where so oft at morn and evening I had watched her
careless play.
On the dark and pine-crowned mountain lies her lonely
little grave,
And for dirge we heard the sea-wind and the beating of
the wave.


"Then for days I lay in fever, shrieking with fierce voice
and wild;
Cursing God and cursing Nature for the deathbed of my
child.
And beneath its weight of sorrow slowly my proud spirit
sank,
Till at last my senses left me and my life became a blank.
.        .        .        .        .        .

"Weak and ill at last I wakened from that dark and
dismal night,
But the world seemed changed around me and the
sunshine lost its light;
And the Springs of Hope were withered, and love's flame
had ceased to burn,
And I knew a power had left me that would never more
return."

## PART II.

### I.

" Changed I was, my love grown colder, vivid fancies
thronged my brain,
Forms and faces hovered round me, and I turned from
them in vain ;
And a madness fired my spirit till I could not bear the
place
Haunted by the tender memory of one little childish face.

" So at last we sold the station, left that wild and rugged
shore,
Changed the calm of Nature's fastness for the busy city's
roar.
For the years had made us wealthy, richer far than those
we met,
And I longed for some excitement that would teach me
to forget.

" In those days of calm seclusion I had thought not of
the worth
Of the royal gift of beauty Nature gave me at my birth.
*Then* a girl unformed and simple, *now* a woman 'midst
my peers,
And my mirror showed my beauty had but ripened with
the years.
What to woman were gold tresses, Grecian face, imperial
form,
But to hold mankind in bondage and to take the world
by storm ?

" Statelier than all women round me, with an air of
careless pride
Little cared I for their hatred with men thronging to my
side.

Still my husband, ever with me, spoke no word and made
no sign
That he knew the gulf was widening fast between his life
and mine.
So I plunged into the vortex of a wild and reckless set,
Ever seeking fresh excitement that would teach me to
forget.


" Was it only sorrow drove me to those scenes with folly
rife ?
Or the thought of something missing in the lottery of
life ?
Often came again the memories of a better, purer day,
When at morn from heated ballrooms swift our carriage
rolled away.
Who shall read a woman's secret ? or divine what women
think ?
One kind word perchance had saved me when I trembled
on the brink,
But his coldness numbed my spirit, and I moved unto my
fate,
Love first changing into friendship, friendship changing
into hate.


" Well I knew my beauty lingered as a theme on every
tongue,
And I learnt to love the homage of the men who round
me hung,
Till the thirst for admiration at last became a daily
need—
Ah ! what misery in the sowing of that single deadly
seed !
Fatal is the gift of beauty to a woman weak and proud ;
Better far for her the features of the homeliest in the
crowd.

Drinking of the wine of flattery till its fumes had turned
my brain,
Thinking only of the worship of the fools who thronged
my train,
Conquest but succeeded conquest when all bowed beneath
my spell,
Till in all the pride and splendour of my vanity——I fell."


II.

" O, fain would I hide
Myself and my shame in the depths of the fathomless sea,
Beneath storm, beyond calm, where no echoes of past days
can be ;
In a tomb deep and wide
Where wrapt in a mantle of darkness and peace I might
slumber afar
From the noise of a world where the voices of Sorrow and
Memory are.

"Hope ! Is there hope ?
Ah ! the hope that shall shine in the gloom of the Valley
of Death ;
Yea ! E'en 'neath the wings of dark Azrael, the chill of
his breath ;
What courage can cope
With Fate when repentance avails not, tho' tears may
have fallen like rain ?
Can the rose that is soiled in the dust of the way its lost
beauty regain ?

" Peace ! Is there Peace ?
Ah ! the peace that is hers whom no woman forgets or
forgives !
The stigma of shame that no penitence ever outlives !
For her shall not cease

2

The frost of contempt and keen words and the stings of
the arrows of scorn.
Ah ! better for her who shall fall in her pride had she
never been born !


"Light !   Is there light
In the deepening of shadows gigantic that gather and
roll—
In the veils of black darkness o'erwhelming the shudder-
ing soul
Like wings of the night ?
Not from man, not from woman, comes mercy to those
who shame's pathway have trod.
Hope, Peace, Light, alone can be found in the infinite
mercy of God.


"O pitiless fate !
O frailty of woman ! that heeds not tho' danger be clear,
That stifles the voices of warning, refusing to hear—
That hears when too late !
Canst thou cleanse the soiled lily of honour by pain and
remorse of long years,
Tho' thou cherish its life with thine anguish and water
its petals with tears ?


"O for pow'r to forget
When Mem'ry is madness, and thought as the stabbing of
swords,
When the sneer of contempt and the lingering sting of
his words
Are haunting me yet !
'I have torn thy false face from my heart, thou art
nothing to me save a name,
And o'er thee shall linger for ever the horror and curse
of thy shame.' .

"Ah ! where shall I find
Some refuge of darkness, some cave of oblivion, deep-
hidden, serene,
Where hushed are the voices of Mem'ry and shades of
the past are unseen,
Where the senses grow blind
'Neath the spell of a peace that is brooding supreme o'er
an echoless shore,
And the dreams of dead hopes and lost honour shall
reach me and haunt me no more ? "

### III.

" How weary the years
To the heart that is reckless of aught that the future may
bring !
That heeds not the glory of summer, the freshness of
spring ;
When sorrow and tears
And the sharp aching throb of remorse burn fiercely like
fire in the brain,
And only the ghosts of past days and the shadow of evil
remain.

. . . . . .

" I have learnt he is dead ;
Nor ever again shall I list to that voice once so tender
and true—
Nor ever again shall I see that strong face which no fear
could subdue.
I have learnt he is dead ;
He has fallen enthroned with the brave in their glory,
yet scorning to yield or to flee,
But breathing no word of forgiveness—and leaving no
message for me.

" I have learnt that he fell
'Midst the storm of the battle that raged far away on the
  hot blinding sand,
Serving unknown in the regiment where once he had
  held a command ;
And the sound of his knell
Was the thunder of cannon, the rattle of bullets swift
  hissing like rain,                        .
And his shroud was the flag he defended—his bier was a
  mound of the slain.


"Methought that I woke
'Midst the combat, and saw the blue gleaming of steel
  bristling bare ;
But haggard and white were the faces that manned the
  four sides of the square ;
Then came the long stroke
Of galloping hoofs shaking earth in their thunder, and
  peal upon peal,
Then the crash and recoil of the squadrons that reeled
  from those walls of blue steel.


" 'Midst murderous rain,
The square closing up, filling gaps made by dying and
  dead,
Returning with volleys defiant each death-dealing chal-
  lenge of lead ;
Then sounded again
The rush of wild steeds, and the redd'ning of sabres, the
  loud grinding shock,
Where alone 'midst the waves of the battle those heroes
  stood firm as a rock.

" Ah ! I saw him still there,
Unmoved 'midst the gleaming of sword play, the can-
non's deep roar,
In one hand the flag that he guarded, in one the long
sabre he wore ;
His thin silver hair
Streamed wild in the breath of the battle, and full on his
resolute face
Was the glow and the light of a spirit that yields not, but
dies in its place.


" But it was not to last,
For swift the dark squadrons had rallied—the square was
a handful of men,
And the strength of the foe unto theirs was e'en greater
than sixty to ten ;
Till, wild as the blast,
One desperate charge overwhelmed them, yet dying they
scorned still to yield,
And fighting they fell at their posts every man—but
mown down like the grass of the field.


" My heart is as stone,
But the tears of my grief will not flow tho' I would I
could weep
For the mem'ry of Love that was tender and faith that
my folly held cheap,
Ah ! too late we own,
With tones of self scorn and upbraiding and pangs of
unquenchable pain
That we know not the worth of a heart till we lose it
and seek it in vain.

" Perchance it is best ;
I have wronged him in thought and in deed by a wrong
   that no tears can repair.
Ah ! would it were *I* and not *he* who was lying in majesty
   there !
He has found a last rest,
He has fallen enthroned with the brave in their glory, yet
   scorning to yield or to flee—
But breathing no word of forgiveness and leaving no
   message for me.

.　　　.　　　.　　　.　　　.　　　.

" O desolate years !
I am weary and stricken, and fain would I lay me at peace
Where the roar of the noise of the world and its follies
   and vanities cease,
   Its hopes and its fears.
Yet one thing remains to a spirit as saddened and hope-
   less as I,
To seek the old home where my darling is sleeping and
   look on her grave ere I die."

PART III.

I.

Night has come ; o'er vale and mountain fast her sable
   robes are sweeping,
Fainter wanes the dying sunlight ling'ring slow by
   shore and lea,
Not a whisper mars the silence round the spot where she
   is sleeping
Save the murmur of the breezes and the music of the
   sea.

With melodious sound and nearer beat the waves with
    ceaseless motion,
  Beat the waves in measured cadence falling on the rocky
    strand,
And the low wind sighs responsive to the rhythm of the
    ocean
  Like the song of some sweet singer echoing thro' a
    dreary land.

All th' immeasurable ether gleams and glows with light
    supernal,
  Glitt'ring points of red and crystal, trembling bars of
    silver white,
Watchfires where the armèd angels guard the throne of
    the Eternal,
  Outposts of a host unnumbered, scattered through the
    Infinite.

    .      .      .      .      .      .

'Tis the grave ; no urn of marble crowns the site with
    classic splendour,
  On the headstone gray and rugged hangs a single faded
    wreath,
Wild flowers round it and above it—emblems of the pure
    and tender—
  None are half so sweet and spotless as the flower that
    lies beneath.

Here, where Peace on wings majestic rules the Night as
    her dominion,
  Watches with her shield of Silence at the grave beside
    the sod,
Dreamlessly the child is sleeping 'neath the shadow of her
    pinion,
  Far from passion, toil, and sorrow ; near to Nature and
    to God.

"Tiny blossom that hath faded ere the summer's noon
and beauty,
Whom an angel's hand hast gathered in the sweetness
of the Spring ;
Little feet that have not learnt to tread the iron path of
Duty,
Have not felt the sword of Sorrow, or the bitter shames
that sting.

"It is better thus, my darling ! Better than a dark to-
morrow
Where the fruits of Love and Pleasure turn to Passion
and Despair,
For the joy of Life is lesser than the burthen of its sorrow,
And I would that God would lay me in the grave beside
you there."

## II.

"Deeper, wider grows the darkness o'er the forest softly
stealing ;
Shadowy trees as dim and gloomy as the shadows they
have thrown
Gird me round with walls Cimmerian as I weep in silence
kneeling
By the grave that holds within it all that I can call
mine own.

"What is Life ? A changeful season—bright to-day and
dark to-morrow ;
Say not : 'Those who sow in anguish shall at last in
gladness reap.'
Rather say : 'The fruits of Folly shall be reaped in pain
and sorrow'—
Then, the voice that all must answer—and the last long
dreamless sleep.

"Hark!  On pinions swift, untiring, sweeping southward,
    sweeping shoreward,
  Over continent and ocean comes the wild wind flying
    fast,
  Like a god he comes to conquer from his Kingdom in the
    Nor'ward,
  And a clarion voice is ringing—'Tis the spirit of the
    blast!


"Hark!  Again that voice, resounding, swells and sinks
    in trembling motion,
  Ringing nearer, ringing clearer, like a sweet-toned silver
    bell,
  'Magdalenè! Magdalenè!' echoing shoreward from the
    ocean—
  'Tis my darling's voice that calls me.  'Tis the voice I
    loved so well.


"Not a sound—the dark trees stir not.  Am I waking?
    Am I dreaming?
  Silence in the shadowy forest, silence in the wilderness,
  But in arching blue above me crystal stars are coldly
    gleaming
  Like the eyes of those who judge me, cruel, stern, and
    pitiless.


"List!  From utter darkness round me once again that
    song sonorous,
  As of those whose souls unfettered soar beyond these
    prison bars,
  Comes, with sound of rushing pinions, voices in celestial
    chorus,
  Mighty waves of deep-toned music rolling heavenwards
    to the stars.

" 'Tis as tho' the skies were sundered and the starry hosts,
    descending,
  Bring the joy of the Immortal to a soul in dark despair,
'Till I hear the mystic echo of those voices strangely
    blending
  Ling'ring in one trembling note, and dying on the
    midnight air !


" But one clear voice dies not ever : over mountain, shore,
    and hollow,
  ' Magdalenè ! Magdalenè ! ' ever calling from the sea.
'Tis my darling's voice that calls me, and with trembling
    steps I follow
  Whereso'er that voice shall lead me till it lead at last
    to Thee."


### III.

Mute she sped ; thro' lonely forests on her feeble foot-
    steps bore her—
  Weird ravines, dim haunted valleys, where the storm
    sprites range and rave,
Till the shelving hills dipt eastward, and she saw at last
    before her,
  Wide and far, a pall of darkness on the sleeping summer
    wave.


Till by yellow sands and shingle, dim dark rocks, gaunt
    cliffs and hoary,
  Stood the woman pale and weeping, with sad heart and
    weary feet,
And the harvest moon arising smote the heavens with
    sudden glory,
  Trembled on the faint horizon where the sky and waters
    meet,

Clothed the misty deep beneath it with a weird and pallid
   splendour,
Shot a ray of stainless silver 'thwart the wave from East
   to West,
Cleft th' empurpled dusk asunder with a radiance white
   and slender,
With a stream that flashed and trembled on the purple
   ocean's breast—


Which to weary eyes that watched it seemed a path to
   Realms Immortal,
Seemed a path of light celestial that the angels might
   have trod,
From the shores beyond the Dawning to the verge of
   Death's dark portal
Leading from this vale of shadows to the Majesty of
   God.


Flash the vaulted heights with brilliance, myriad gems
   that gleam and quiver,
And the ocean's shining bosom mirrors clear the
   jewelled dome !
" Heaven above and heaven beneath me ; and beyond—
   the silver river—
Still she calls me .   . 'Magdalenè !' .   . Darling
   —I am coming home."


Then the clarion voice vibrated over ocean, shore, and
   hollow—
" Magdalenè ! Magdalenè "—ever calling from the sea ;
And she answered, "I am ready.   Onward ! Onward !   I
   will follow
Wheresoe'er thy voice shall lead me till it lead at last
   to Thee."

From her soul she felt the burden of her sorrow slip and
sever,
  As the mists disperse and vanish, fading at the face of
Day ;
All the passion and the fever of the brain were gone for
ever—
  All the fierce unrest and longing sank in peace and
passed away.


IV.

"I am bound by a power that is deathless, a yearning
divine
That draws my soul onward, resistless, my child, unto
thine,
That lifts my sad heart with a gladness unspoken to thee,
            Thy voice from the sea.


"Lo ! the shame and the shadow of sin that lay dark on
my breast
They have lifted and vanished as mists from the blue
mountain's crest
Thro' the silence of death, thro' the gloom and the glory
of Night,
            I shall pass into light.


"Thy voice like the sound of sweet melody trembles and
falls,
Thy voice like the peal of the clarion thrills me and
calls—
Calls me to thee at the gates of High Heaven in the
Realms of the Blest—
            And I pass to my rest."

And as one who moves and gazes fixed and silent in her
  dreaming,
With a step that did not falter and a heart that did not
  shrink,
Like a goddess in the moonlight, with her fair hair round
  her gleaming,
Passionless, erect, and stately, passed she, slowly, to the
  brink.


With her blue eyes wide and dreamy, golden locks around
  her clinging,
Bride of Death and crowned with beauty fair as hers
  whose name she bore,
Following onward, following ever, where that clarion
  voice was ringing,
Down the calm and silver river passed she, silent, from
  the shore.


Deeper, deeper, grew the waters closing round her and
  above her,
Dimmer grew the dusky shore-line fading faintly in the
  West,
Till the purple star-flushed ocean clasped her to him like
  a lover,
Drew her in his strong embrace, and hid her, sleeping,
  in his breast.


But the Night-breeze blowing shoreward bore a sound
  o'er vale and hollow,
" Magdalenè ! Magdalenè ! " ever calling from the sea,
And the trembling echo answered, " Onward ! Onward !
  I will follow
Wheresoe'er thy voice shall lead me till it lead at last
  to Thee."

# THE BLACK KNIGHT.

FIERCE were the feuds on the Borderland
   When the sword was Law in the days of old,
When the world was ruled by the mailèd hand,
   And the might to seize was the right to hold.

In the gory tracks of the War God's feet
   Rapine and Terror came following fast,
As each slumbering town and peaceful street
   Awoke to the sound of the trumpet's blast.

*Then* the day was bright with the glint of arms ;
   *Then* the night was red with the fires that leapt
From burning hamlets and wasted farms
   Where the ruthless floods of invasion swept.

From across the Tweed came the clansmen bold,
   And Northumberland's spearsmen barred the way ;
But an English Earl lay rigid and cold
   Ere the Borderers fled from that deadly fray.

    .     .     .     .     .     .     .

Three years rolled onward, and Time had spread
   A mantle of peace by the Northern rills ;
No trumpet's blast and no martial tread
   Woke the echoing voice of the slumb'ring hills.

On the armoury wall hung the tall war-shield,
And the good sword rusted within its sheath,
And the knights who charged on the battle-field
Now followed the chase o'er the purple heath.

　　.　　.　　.　　.　　.　　.　　.

But again they come !  From across the Tweed
Rush the lawless Borderers forth to war ;
With gath'ring strength and with stealthy speed
They march 'neath the light of the morning star,

Till the gleaming line of their battle-van
By noonday breaks thro' the leafy wood,
And the message speeds onward from man to man :-
" The castle is girt by the Northern brood ! "

Then spreads a tumult of fierce surprise
And swords are girded with stern intent
As the creaking drawbridge upward flies
And the archers rush to the battlement.

In the spacious hall of that castle gray
Sat the widowed Countess whose noble lord
Was slain in the arms of Victory
Three summers since by a Northern sword.

Ah !  Too well she guessed as she heard the din
The dire import of that echoing shout,
The tramp of the armoured guard within
And the rattle of shafts on the walls without.

As she sped from the hall to the ramparts high,
Where the faithful ranks of her vassals stood,
All hearts beat fast as she passed them by
In the pride of her perfect womanhood.

Like a vision of beauty in dreamland born
  She stood in the midst of those mail-clad knights
As a wild flower blooms in the bearded corn,
  Or a bright star gleams in the misty heights.
But white was her cheek as the driven snow
  Ere its mantle covers the Autumn leaves,
And her dark eyes shone with feverish glow
  As she glanced t'wards the Northern helms and greaves.
Then she spake to the Chief of that silent band,
  Who stood sternly watching the moving foe,
While the good swords shone in each knight's right hand,
  And the shaft on the string of each archer's bow :
" Speak !   Where is the boy ? "   Not a voice replied ;
  Not a warrior stirred ; but from face to face
There flashed the dread which they could not hide—
  " *In the ruthless hands of that hated race !* "

          .       .       .       .       .       .       .

" I come from the Chiefs who have crossed the Tweed,
  And I speak in the words which they spake to me,
Yield the castle up : drop the bridge with speed,
  Or the boy shall swing on the nearest tree."

Then answered Humont of Chillingham Keep
  (The dead Earl's brother), and roundly swore,
Till the castle walls were a ruined heap
  To fight for the monarch whose badge he wore.

A more fearless heart on a battle plain
  Beat not in Britain or north of the Tweed,
But his mind was made of a warlike grain,
  And his faith was the faith of the Spartan Creed.

" Go hence, Sir Herald, to whence ye came,
  And tell the Chiefs of yon Northern horde
That they who dare offer such terms of shame
  Shall find reply at the point of the sword ;

And if but one hair of the young child's head
  Be harmed by them—then for every hair
A Northumbrian blade shall gleam blood-red,
  When Humont of Chillingham storms their lair."

Then the Countess, turning her troubled eyes,
  Spake with trembling lips, and with gesture wild ;
" Will ye stand and look while my darling dies ?
  I love my king, but—O, my child ! my child ! "

But they looked at the forest of spears which shone
  On the plain beneath, and their bold hearts fell
At such terrible odds.   Oh ! was there none
  Who would save the boy whom she loved so well ?

There was one !   He had loved with a hopeless love,
  Had loved her as maid, and widow, and wife,
With a faith as pure as the stars above,
  The one pure faith of a sinful life.
For his youth had been wild, and his hands were red
  With the blood of crime, and the fearful fame
Of his prowess and lawless deeds had spread
  Till the Border rang with his hated name—
The Black Knight, Conrad, whose sword and plume
  When far in the battle they gleamed and tossed
On the field where the brave Earl met his doom
  Had turned the tide when the day seemed lost.
Dark was that plume as the raven's wing,
  Black was his armour from head to heel,
And the two-edged sword none but he could swing
  Was wrought and fashioned of bluest steel.
His face was pale, but it was not fear
  That had blanched the bronze on his rugged cheek,
But a passion that told in a single tear
  The depth of a thought which he could not speak,

3

From its sable sheath leapt his shining sword ;
  By the cross of its hilt and by Holy Rood
He swore he would wrest from that savage horde
  The only joy of her widowhood.

Then he looked at the faces that burnt with shame ;
  And the hosts of the North he gazed upon ;
And he said, as his colour went and came :
  " They have slain the sire ; shall they slay the son ? "

The Countess heard ; and her heart was sore
  With mingled sorrow and joy and pride
As she thought of the love she had scorned before
  And the faith of a heart she had cast aside.
She strove to speak, but she strove in vain ;
  She strove to move, but her limbs seemed stone ;
And her bosom heaved like the troubled main
  When its surface is ruffled and tempest-blown.
And the passion that swelled in her tender breast
  Had made her face like the face of the dead
As her hand to his bearded lips he prest
  And passed from her sight with a steady tread.

          .     .     .     .     .     .     .

Then the Black Knight turned and with steady hand
  Filled the crystal goblet and raised it high
Till it glittered and flashed like a shining brand
  In the mellow light, as he made reply :

" 'Thro' the lists of Life rides an Unseen Knight
  On a phantom steed from the Realms of Gloom,
And he challenges all to stand and fight
  Ere they pass thro' the gates of the silent Tomb.
What matters it then, since we all must fall
  At the fatal thrust of his viewless spear,
If I meet him now 'neath the castle wall
  For the sake of the boy whom she holds so dear ?

I have charged ere now at the bristling banks
  Of a steel-blue line when all hope seemed wild ;
I will tilt with Death in the Northern ranks
  For the pure young life of this fair-haired child.
Fill the goblet up with the blood-red wine,
  Be it Life ! be it Death ! we are comrades true,
Drink thou to my sword in the battle-line !
  I will pledge the sweet face which I leave with you ! "


With the drawbridge down, and the postern wide,
  And a steady grip on the bridle-rein—
One touch of the spur to the stallion's side,
  And he shot like a bolt for the open plain.
With his visor barred, and his broadsword freed,
  And his black plume tossed in the wind's strong breath,
When the long low strides of the gallant steed
  Beat stronger, faster, he rode to his death.
Breathless they watched from the plain—from the gate,
  Both friends and foemen struck dumb to see
One warrior charging fearless and straight
  The deep ranks of the Northern chivalry.
From the plain—from the gate—from the castle roofs
  No sound was borne on the balmy gale
Save the echoing thud of galloping hoofs
  And the clank of the rider's sable mail.
He crashed thro' the ranks of that armoured band
  Ere a sword was drawn or a shaft had sped,
Till he reached the tree where a cruel hand
  Had just swung the boy to a branch o'erhead.
One circling flash of the shining blade
  And the cord was cut and the boy was free—
One strong bold reach with his arms he made,
  And the child sat firm on his saddle-tree.
Then broke the thunder of falling blows,
  As they rained like hail on his sable gear ; -

And the gleam of his sword as it fell and rose,
    And the ring of his war-cry proudly clear.
And louder and louder the tumult roared,
    And brighter and brighter fresh steel flashed forth,
As high in the midst of that savage horde
    His dark plume waved o'er the crests of the North.
And swift was the hiss of his Southern sword
    As it swung like a reed in his strong right hand,
And short was the shrift of each warlike lord,
    If it beat down the guard of his Northern brand.
Beneath the shade of his tall black shield
    He covered the boy on his saddle bow,
And the strength of a nature that could not yield
    Gave nerve to his arm and illumined his brow.
But the odds were long and the strife was sore,
    And thrice in the conflict they saw him reel,
And thrice the crest that ne'er bent before
    Was lost to their sight in that sea of steel.
But ever it rose !   At his terrible tilt
    The Borderers shrank till his broadsword good,
Erst blue as the river, from point to hilt
    Was crimson and dripping with Northern blood.
Quoth the seneschal on the castle wall ;
    " No blade in Britain this day could stand
'Gainst such frightful odds.   The boy must fall
    With the bravest heart in our native land."
But, maddened to frenzy, he charged again ;
    The black steed sprang to the spurrèd heel ;
He thrust to the heart and he clove to the brain
    Wherever he struck, as he cleared a lane.
To the right, to left, the Borderers reel
    At the terrible sweep of that dripping steel.
And the weight and strength of the brave black steed
    And the cut and thrust that was sure and straight
Broke through their ranks, and at headlong speed
    He raced once more for the castle gate.

But she who watched from the battlement
  Had seen with growing terror, and wild,
That his gear was stained and his armour bent,
  And he swayed in his seat as he held the child.
Till his face grew white with a sudden pain
  As he fell to the ground with a hollow groan,
And the maddened steed with a trailing rein
  Bore the child to the castle gate alone.
Then strong as the tide of the torrent sets
  Was the rush of the North on its helpless prey ;
But the hurtling hail from the parapets
  Guarded the ground where the Black Knight lay.
While the cross-bow shafts were as deadly rain
  They bore him in whom no fear could quell,
And the clank of the bridge as it rose again
  Smote on their hearts like a funeral knell.
All bruised and bleeding they bore him in,
  And they knew as they bore him that ne'er again
Would his broadsword clash in the steel-rung din,
  Or his war-cry float o'er the battle plain.

    .      .      .      .      .      .      .

The pure white flame of a deathless love
  Burnt in his soul, and his brow grew bright
With a radiance that seemed to the eyes above
  Like a faint reflex of celestial light,
Till the waves of passion lashed high and broke
  Over his soul in a stemless tide,
And rushed to the cold blue lips and spoke
  With the strength of a love which he could not hide :

" I have loved the clash of the ringing steel
  When it gleams blood-red in the mailèd hand,
And the crash of the charge when the riders reel,
  And the short sharp tones of the stern command ;

The brunt of the battle—when deadlocks hold
    The steeds and the riders in grappling vice,
Where the hate is bitter, and hearts are bold,
    And a faulty thrust is not given twice.
I have loved the bay of the deep-mouthed hound,
    And the mellow swell of the bugle horn,
When the short green sward was a jewelled ground
    With the diamond dew of the early morn.
I have done with the chase and the martial strife,
    And I crave them not, for thy dark eye saith
That the love which I could not win in life
    Shall be mine for ever, my love, in death.
Bend down thy dark and sorrowful eyes
    Till the burning rays of their light illume
The vapours of Death, and the mysteries
    Of the path which lies thro' the gates of gloom.
O clasp me still closer to thee, and lay
    My sinking head on thy trembling breast !
I had prayed to fall where the broadswords play,
    But to breathe my last in thine arms is best.
With the blood of crime has my hand been stained ;
    My faults are many, and virtues few,
But one light that never wavered or waned
    Was the guiding star of my love for you.
And it may be yet in that Unknown Land,
    Where my soul, ere long, shall have entered in,
That a true deed done by a strong right hand
    May balance the weight of a life of sin.
My heart throbs slow with a tremulous beat,
    The words I would utter sound faint and low ;
But the touch of your warm red lips is sweet,
    And whisper you love me before I go.
I have played my part in the world of strife,
    And why should I linger for lesser bliss ?
Ah ! what now are the years of a misspent life
    To one single hour of a death like this ? "

# JOHN RAEBURN.

## I.

" DEAD ! Who says she is dead ? . . . I hold his letter
before mine eyes.
Gone from the Valley of Shadows to the light of ineffable
skies !
He writes ' She is dead,' and I know of no cause to
suspect that he lies.

" He writes ' She is dead ! ' and the light of a hope that
I dreamt would not die
Has flickered and waned into darkness and left but the
pitiful cry :
' God gathers the flowers that are purest and best and
thou shalt not ask why.'

" Not dead ! for the soul is immortal.  She lives where
these eyes cannot see,
And I sit here alone in the silence, and commune,
O Sorrow, with Thee.
But living or dead, till I cease to be, she can never, never
be dead to me.

.        .        .        .        .        .        .

" Who shall write with a fearless hand the secret
thoughts of his inmost soul ?—
Bare his thoughts to the common gaze like written
words on an open scroll ?—
Tell of the fever of passionate love that none can
conquer and few control ?

"Who shall judge by the outward man what the inner
    life of that man may be ?—
Judge of the currents that dart beneath by the placid
    breast of the sleeping sea ?—
Read the truth of the things we see not by the light of
    the things we see ?


"Sweet yet sad seem the days long gone when Youth
    looked round on the world and said :
'See how the garden of Life is garnished with lilies
    white and with roses red.'
Ne'er a thought of the autumn winds when leaves are
    scattered and flowers are dead.


"Years have rolled, but it seems not so, since first I came
    from the mother-land,
Since the day I wandered down by the sea and heard the
    waves beat loud on the sand.
Who shall say the trifles of Life are not the work of an
    Unseen Hand ?


"The Unseen Hand of a changeless Fate that bends our
    souls to a Higher Will,
That gathers lives from North and South for the destiny
    they must each fulfil,
From Life, thro' Death, to that Unknown Land—the
    goal and zenith of good or ill.


"Ah ! Trifles in Life, tho' we heed them not, are
    stoutest links in the brittle chain.
We heed them not, but they bind us fast, with a clasp we
    can never break again,
Their silken weft has the strength of steel, tried in sorrow
    and proved in pain.

" Hers was fair as an angel's face in its passionless calm
    and its sweet repose,
And I stood and watched the gentle heave of her tender
    breast as it fell and rose
Like lazy waves on a summer sea when winds are dying
    and silence grows.

" She had fallen asleep on the yellow sand where the
    sunshine played with her golden hair,
And the heavy fringe of her eyelids drooped on a cheek
    as pure as the lilies fair,
And over all hung the shadow of Peace and the scent
    of the sea-weed everywhere.

" Why tell the tale that was never new since man's first
    love to the world was told ?
The songs which the poets sing to-day are but the songs
    which they sang of old,
Yet the theme will live in its deathless bloom when
    hands are withered and hearts are cold.

" We dreamt in those days of a faith too deep, of Love
    made stronger than Death can be,
And our souls were filled with a passionate fire that
    surged and swelled like a southern sea ;
Tho' bitter the hour of our parting proved, she
    whispered, ' My soul is given to thee ! '

" Far out West, where the breath of the wind is as the
    blast from a furnace mouth,
I made my home in the wilderness, in the land of fever
    and fiery drouth ;
But my soul was hers and it lingers still by the breezy
    shore of the pleasant South.

"I have borne the damp of the chill morass and the
burning heat of the tropic day,
Five years have I toiled for the woman I love with a faith
that Time shall ne'er decay,
Fortune has smiled on my strong right hand ; but all
that I care for has passed away.

"Too late I learn all her heart concealed.   ' Too late ! too
late ! ' the Echo saith.
Her letters ceased as her hand grew weak, and fainter and
fainter her parting breath.
The beauty she wore as a royal robe, alas ! was the fatal
beauty of Death.

" She is gone ! with her heavenly face and the voice that
rang out over the sea ;
And I sit here alone in the silence and commune,
O Sorrow, with Thee.
But, living or dead, till I cease to be she can never, never
be dead to me."

II.

" Three years since she died ! and Time has calmed the
first wild fever of grief and pain,
The wound has partly healed, tho' I deemed such
sorrow could never find peace again,
For the sword struck deep to mine inmost soul, and the
scar will ever remain.

" Do I love her less in these days ?   Not so, for her
memory still is a sacred thing ;
Often methinks I hear her voice in the mystic chants
that the wild winds sing
When they sigh thro' the forest and over the plain
like the moan of a spirit wandering.

"Times have changed, for the tide of Progress, rolling
  westward, has reached me here ;
I have crept from my shell, and mixed with men, and
  grown more kindly and less austere ;
Can it be that the spell of the buried Past is slowly
  lessening year by year ?


" Few are the friends I can call my own, but one have
  I found out here in the West,
And a truer nobler heart than his never beat in a human
  breast ;
Our stations join and my happiest hours are spent with
  him as a welcome guest.


" A gaunt old man with a kingly face and a daughter
  fresh as an English May ;
Like summer and winter they seem to me—the dark
  brown locks and the silver gray.
Let me search my soul—Is it friendship alone that draws
  my steps so oft that way ?


" Brown-eyed Edith—a child of Nature—free as the air
  of her native strand ;
There are few as fair, there are none more true, none
  gentler, none sweeter in all the land ;
But she lacks the grace, the imperial ease, of her I found
  asleep on the sand.


" Child ! if Love should come thy way and whisper low
  with his rosebud mouth—
Breathe on thy soul with the fire of his breath as fierce
  and strong as the wind of the Drouth—
Ah ! thou wilt love with the passionate love that is born
  of the sun and the South !

" Am I false in my thoughts to her who said, soft in my
  ear, ' All my soul is thine ! '
False ! whilst I see, thro' the haze of the past, the deathless eyes of my Margaret shine—
My dead love's eyes as I saw them last, lit with the light
  of a love divine ?

.    .    .    .    .    .    .

" Have I grown vain with the rolling years ? or have
  I read her secret aright ?
Why has she grown so silent and strange ?   Why were
  there tears in her eyes last night ?
Can it be *love* that flushes her cheek, then turns its
  damask to deadly white ?


" Can it be true that Edith loves—loves with a passion as
  fierce and free
As that which shook the strength of my youth, years
  ago, by the sunny sea ?
Have I pierced to the depths of her soul and read that
  she loves—*loves me ?*


" Ah ! I am sick of this lonely life ; faint with the stress
  of these weary days.
I am growing gray in the wilderness ; quaint, old-
  fashioned, in all my ways.
Can it be there is happiness yet hidden deep 'neath the
  shadowy haze ?


" Can I go to her now, look in her eyes, fearlessly take
  her hand in mine ?
And say those words which I said but once, ' O my love,
  all my soul is thine ! '
Hypocrite !   No ; for the eyes of the Dead gaze on this
  life from the Life Divine ! "

III.

"Married ! Is it the hand of Fate ? Edith and I are married at last !
Two quiet years of wedded life and I still clasp my sorrowful secret fast.
I have steeled my heart, I have said to my soul, ' It is time to bury the Past.'

" Do I give to her as honest a love as the faithful homage she pays to me ?
She is all that is womanly, tender, and true ; she is all that a wife should be.
Trustful heart, couldst thou read my thoughts how would thy husband appear to thee ?

" Two years have flown since we stood together, sad and silent, the night he died—
Stood by his couch and watched his life ebbing away like a falling tide.
Friend ! Thou hast passed thro' the River of Death : is there joy and peace on the farther side ?

.  .  .  .  .  .  .

" He whispered softly,—I scarce could hear—he placed her delicate hand in mine,
' Raeburn,' he said, with his dying breath, ' guard her, love her, this trust is thine !
Take my wildflower unto thy heart. Thou art the oak and she is the vine.'

" Poor child ! Poor child, with her passionate heart !
Bitter and wild were the tears she shed. ;
I folded her trembling form to my breast, tender and few were the words I said.
In that darksome room our troth was plighted—hers and mine—alone with the dead.

"I stood with her at the altar of God, I swore the vow
   and I bent the knee,
But I heard a voice that she could not hear, and I saw
   a face that she could not see ;
For Memory rose from the Shadowy Past and stood like
   a spectre over me.

.    .    .    .    .    .    .

"Am I to waste my life in dreams till Death shall me in
   his arms enfold ?
Better to turn to the new love glowing than muse in
   silence over the old,
Better to bury my hopeless grief deep in the grave where
   her heart lies cold !

"Lo ! I will cast off, for ever and ever, all that has held
   my spirit in thrall.
I will taste of the wine and honey of life ; I have lived
   too long on the wormwood and gall.
I have done with the Past.  I have severed the chain.
   I will turn to Edith as all in all.

"Margaret ! hear—if the dead can hear the sighs of our
   souls in that Life above—
Where thou standest—an angel of God—beneath the
   wings of His brooding Dove !
Shall I not cleave to this womanly heart ?  Have I not
   vowed to cherish and love ?

"Passionate love will last for a season, wither the heart
   and weary the breast ;
Is the prize for which we have striven worth all the fever
   of fierce unrest ?
Love that flows like a summer river, musical, passionless,
   is the best.

"Time the Merciful, Time the Healer, who takest the
sting of our sorrows away
And calmest all the unsatisfied longing, surely thou sayest
to all to-day :
'Brood no more on the things that have perished, grasp
your happiness while you may.'

"Truth sits enthroned on her pure white brow, and
Honour shines in her clear brown eyes ;
What tho' she hide the depth of her love beneath the
mask of a sober guise,
Is not the faith of a heart like hers more sweet than all
passionate memories ? "

IV.

"The Morn has come in his glorious sheen of royal
crimson and silver-gray,
And the wings of Night are spread for flight before the
shield of the armèd Day,
And the face of the Earth is lit with joy and the hills are
flushed with a roseate ray.

" For he comes like a lover whom Fate has held far away
from his loved one's side,
And his eyes are keen with the fire of his thoughts and
the fever of longings unsatisfied ;
He comes in the passion and pride of his strength to clasp
the Earth as a bride.

"Fresh and blithe is the morning air, the dew still
glitters on grass and tree ;
And the mystic spell of the wilderness, the charm of the
Bush, creeps over me.
There are times when a man can say to his soul : 'It is
happiness only *to be !* '

" There is peace around, there is peace in my heart, as I
   drive alone thro' the silent land,
And mark once more that the Drouth is o'er and Nature,
   stretching a gracious hand,
Hath changed bare plains into pastures green as tho' by
   the wave of a fairy's wand.


" There is peace in my heart, and a sense of joy thrills my
   being and fills my breast ;
After the grief and tension of passion Happiness comes as
   a welcome guest ;
After the turmoil of weary years God has given me quiet
   and rest.


" Ah ! What is that yonder ?   I know those horses—the
   blue-roan colts that I sold to Gray !
The Dalmora buggy, with the old man and Walter !
   What can be bringing them down to-day ?
They seem in trouble—two traces broken—and the wheels
   gone down in that bed of clay.


" ' I'm afraid that I shall not be able to help you.   I can
   give you this cord to splice up the gear.
It only requires a little patience and those two colts will
   soon pull you clear.
Yes.   I must hurry on to the Five-mile.   Caxton, of
   Woodside, is coming here.


" ' What did you say ?   You are going there also ?   Some
   one expecting—waiting—for you ?
A governess coming up from the South ?   She will find
   this Western life something new.
I will tell her, then, from you if I see her that you will be
   there in an hour or two.'

"Caxton not come ? Without writing to tell me ? Well!
I will trust in his promise no more.
Where can this governess be whom they spoke of? I can
see some one there thro' the open door.
I suppose I had better go in and explain the reason why
Gray was not here before."

## V.

" I enter the room of the little inn—some one is standing
over there,
Her face in the shadow, half turned away. I can only see
she is tall and fair,
For the room seems dark as I pass within, and my eyes
are dazed by the noontide glare.

" Something familiar about the face ! Calmly she moves
out into the light.
Why does she suddenly tremble and start? Why does
her cheek turn deadly white ?
We stand and gaze in each other's eyes, and a mist arises
before my sight.

" We stand and gaze, but we do not speak, for the shadow
of Fate hangs overhead,
And I see once more those deep sad eyes, and the graceful
curve of that stately head.
Has she risen again in the beauty of old ?—'Mine own
true love !—Not dead !—Not dead ! '

" She has come to me thro' the gates of Death, and her
eyes are wet with the angels' tears ;
And Heaven shall mourn—there are none more pure in
all the throng of her starry peers.
She has loved with the strength of a deathless love thro'
all the grief of the bitter years.

4

" Ah ! I forget those weary years, the sword of Sorrow,
the secret pain,
I only know that I clasp her now—mine own true love—
in these arms again.
' O Queen of my soul ! Lift up thine eyes ! Who but
thee in my heart could reign ? '


" She pillows her golden head on my breast, she lifts up
her radiant eyes to mine,
And I feel the sense of their mystic power mount thro'
my brain like the fumes of wine.
They have not changed. They are still the same. Lit
with the light of a love divine.


" It is all a dream that we parted, love. We are sitting
again on the yellow sand ;
We hear the boom of the bursting surf ; we see the white
foam flung on the strand.
It is all a dream that we parted, love. Who was it spoke
of the Western land ?

.        .        .        .        .        .        .


" What do I say ? No dream ! No dream, but the iron
hand 'neath the velvet glove—
The iron Hand of that Destiny decreed by the Unseen
Powers above ! . . .
If loyal to Love, disloyal to Honour—untrue to all I have
sworn to love !


" Deep and wide is the gulf that parts us. All my gain
shall but end in loss.
Thou and I on opposite banks must watch the waters eddy
and toss !
Thou and I on opposite banks—but we may not cross—
but we may not cross !

"Who shall comfort the comfortless, breathe peace to
the heart that is desolate ?
Sin to covet forbidden fruit ! and sin to strive 'gainst the
hand of Fate !
Given me back from the mouth of the grave——given
me back—Too late—Too late !

.    .    .    .    .    .    .

" She has told me all.   I can see the truth.   'Tis written
with fire on my heart and brain.
Our letters passed thro' a villain's hands.   He sold his
honour her love to gain.
He said ' He is dead,' and he wrote me a lie.   We believed,
and we never wrote again.

" He loved her then ?   Was this the friendship he swore
to me in the days that were ?
I would give the years I have yet to live only to see him
standing there,
To meet him alone——Be his strength what it may, I am
armed with the strength of mine own despair.

" We two alone where no ear could hear !   We two alone
where no eye could see !
Mercy !   Yea, I would mete to him the mercy he rendered
to mine and me.
I would shoot him there like a dog where he stood, tho' I
passed with him to Eternity."

VI.

"Going to Dalmora !   *She*, the new governess !   *She !*
with her beauty of mind and face,
Waiting there where the coach had left her.   Why was
she not met at the place ?
Ah ! I remember.   To think that our meeting was brought
about by a broken trace !

"Trifles! This is how Fate impending works great issues
from little things,
A random blow on a wound half healed, and Hope falls
stricken with trailing wings.
Trifles! a careless stroke of the pick may strike the gold,
or the hidden springs.

.    .    .    .    .    .    .

"Now, I am calm. I stand once more encased in mine
armour of self-control.
Could I stem the rush of the pent-up passion surging as
waves of the Tempest roll?
When all things else were as things forgotten, and each
sought each with the eyes of the soul!

"Back to the station! In these few hours how all the
current of life has changed,
Flowing again in the old old channels, the hills and
valleys where once it ranged.    ·
Back to the station! Back to Edith, with courage failing
and faith estranged!

" To live so close—scarce twenty miles—and all our meet-
ings but grief and pain.
So near, yet so far—parted for ever. Did she not say,
' We have severed the chain ;
The Past is buried ; the book is closed, *never*, friend, to
be opened again ' ?

"Back to the station! to take up once more the quiet
routine of daily life.
How can I look with a fearless gaze into the faithful eyes
of my wife,
The truest, tenderest wife on earth, who shall never know
of this inward strife ? "

VII.

" Am I so weak that I cannot say, 'I will be true whatsoe'er betide,
True in action and true in thought'? Have I no honour,
no manly pride?
Yes. I will honour and love to the last the woman whose
place must be at my side.

" Ah! but Love is not governed by Will. Love has no
law. 'Tis unfettered and free.
Canst thou stand on the yellow sand and curb the tide of
the rising sea? . . .
. . . Get thee behind me, Satan, for ever. . . . Tempt
me no more in my misery.

.     .     .     .     .     .     .

" Edith and she are the closest friends. She has ridden
down to Dalmora to-day.
She likes her better than any one else. 'We must have
the new governess over to stay,
So sweet and so sad. Such a beautiful face.' I answer
and laugh in a careless way.

.     .     . .     .     .     .     .

" She has come to my home, she is under my roof. My
heart beats fast as I touch her glove!
Grown so fragile she seemeth to me like an angel sent
from the Heavens above.
I see them yonder standing together—my wife and the
woman I love.

" No! Not love! I have crushed the memory. Edith,
alone, until Time shall end.
I, too, can turn from fruit forbidden ; I, too, can accept
what Fate may send.
'The Past is buried ; the book is closed, never again to
be opened, friend!'"

VIII.

"It is better to die, better to sleep, to lay down one's
   burden and be at rest,
To cast off for ever the shackles of sorrow, the passions
   and sins of a troubled breast,
To cross the bounds of the darksome river.   Death is not
   terrible.   Death is best.

"I am spent with the struggle that rends my spirit and
   leaves me far from the wished-for goal—
Faint with the effort to curb and weaken the strength of
   the passions I cannot control,
'Whilst Love and Honour like mailèd knights contend for
   the prize of my soul.

"Why should I strive to deceive myself?   Sophist! thy
   platitudes are but vain !
Turn as thou wilt from the days that were, truth will
   triumph and truth will reign.
No ! Thou canst *never* bury the past.   No ! Thou canst
   *never* unrivet the chain.

"Then it were wiser to seek a haven where Memory's
   echoes no more shall mock,
Wiser to grasp the buckler and halberd and close with
   Death in a mortal shock !
The Coward's refuge !—I will not seek it——   The Rae-
   burns come of a different stock ! "

.     .     .     .     .     .     . .

Here the diary ends ; for the hand that had written, wrote
   no more on the page of Time.
It is only the tale of two ruined lives ; and one has passed
   to a happier clime—
Passed from the feverish dreams of Earth to the widening
   vistas of Life sublime.

.     .     .     .     .     .     .

IX.

They found him lying—a shattered wreck—'neath splin-
tered woodwork and broken wheel,
And his face was pale as the face of one on whom Death's
Angel has set his seal,
But life still throbbed in the sinking frame, in the flaccid
muscles once strong as steel.

. . . . . . .

" Bend closer, Edith. Don't cry, my darling !—Death
must come to us all some day—
Who will guard you and who will keep you now that I
am going away ?
Closer, Edith—— I am growing fainter—— There is
something yet that I wish to say.

" There is a book—a diary,—— Burn it !—Some things
are better lost in the grave !
Promise me you will never read it. I have tried to be
true—— I have tried to be brave——
Have I failed in my duty to you, my darling ?—— Have
I failed to fulfil the trust he gave ?

" Ah ! but who is that standing there ?—— Have you
brought her to see me before I die ?——
Kiss me, Edith—— The shadows deepen——the light
has faded out of the sky——
Margaret—give me your hand again—— The Past is
buried—Good-bye—— Good-bye !" . . .

. . . . . . .

Two women are sitting, side by side ; they watch the
shadows that play on the wall,
And the darkness is creeping up from the East to cover
the Earth like a funeral pall ;
No voice is heard by the listening air and the silence of
Death broods over it all.

Deep are the thoughts in the heart of each—thoughts
  which they feel yet never shall say ;
Hand in hand they sit in the silence till Dawn has come
  in his mantle of gray ;
But they know that their souls are bound together by the
  strength of a bond that will not decay.

.          .          .          .          .          .          .

He has fallen asleep, he is buried deep in his lonely grave
  'neath the Western sod ;
He will tread no more on that Unknown Shore the path
  of Sorrow his feet have trod ;
He has passed to the realms of Eternal Peace " where they
  are as the Angels of God."

# AN ECHO.

In the harmony of ages floating from the dreamy Past,
In the old romantic legends where the seeds of song were
cast,
In the pleasant fields of Fancy, whence the flowers of
genius sprung,
Can we find a path untrodden ?   Can we find a song
unsung ?
Lamps of Genius burning brightly thro' the mists of
bygone days,
With the light of strong endeavour ever mingling with
their rays ;
Dreams of dreamers, chants of singers made immortal in
their song,
With a soft and tender cadence, or a passion fierce and
strong,
Like the chimes from distant belfries, like the restless
winds that blow
Northwards with tempestuous fury, southwards musically
slow ;
Like the thunderous roar of breakers bursting on a rocky
strand,
Or the rhythm of the river murmuring softly thro' the
land ;
Sinking, rising, soaring upwards sound their melodies
sublime—
Sound the Voices of the Ages echoing thro' the Halls of
Time.

What is left us ?  Shall we wander midst the fields their
  feet have prest ?
Sing again the songs they sang us in their passion of
  unrest ?
Sing of Nature, 'neath whose influence all the poet's
  instinct stirs—
Feels the throbbing of his pulses beat in unison with
  hers ;
When the Dawn's grey veil of vapour falls before the
  face of Day,
And the arrows of the sunshine chase the shadowy night
  away ;
Like a goddess in her splendour, robed with many a
  roseate hue,
In the mantle of the morning, jewelled with the glittering
  dew ?
Softer is the calm of sunset, mellower light on plain
  and tree,
Placid purple clouds, like islands floating in a golden sea,
When the crimson-tinted sunlight sinks and pales in
  waning rays,
And like rush of many waters, come the thoughts of
  other days ;
Till the creeping mists grow deeper and the evening air
  is still
With the awe of solemn shadows hanging darkly on the
  hill ;
Till with wide and rapid pinions sweeps the Spirit of the
  Night,
And our thoughts are carried onwards in the current of
  its flight,
Through the wreathing mists of darkness where the mid-
  night reigns alone
From the regions of the Finite to the bars of the Un-
  known.

All our songs are but the echoes of the chants long
  heard before,
All our loves and our ambitions like the wave-beats on
  the shore,
Coming, going, passing, ending with their restless hopes
  and fears,
Till at last in silence buried in the cenotaph of years.

# EVENING : A FRAGMENT.

THIS is the hour of Rest ! Nature doth sleep,
Draped in the shadowy garments of the night,
And from the vast immeasurable height,
The stars of Heaven their silent vigils keep,
The emblems of Eternity. They stand,
God's sentinels, without the gates of Heaven.
This is the hour of Peace ! There is no sound.
The fitful voices of the wandering winds
Have died in hollow murmurs. Near and far
Upon the sleeping Earth, beneath, around ;
Descends the mantle of a deeper calm.
It is the Spirit of the Night that speaks—
" A still, small voice "—but with a magic power
It sinks into the heart, till the wild wars
Of earthly passions and corroding cares
Disperse like clouds before the rising sun.
This is the hour of Thought ! In this still hour
The nature we inherit from High God,
In conflict with our baser attributes,
Rises triumphant, bidding us prepare
For holier thoughts and higher destinies.
O Man ! If thou wouldst gauge thy littleness,
And know thine impotency, go behold
The stars of Heaven ! For if thy mind conceives,
And counts them held by beings such as we,
With hopes, ambitions, loves, akin to ours,
In what proportion dost thou find thyself

To the united millions of all worlds ?
One single grain in miles of desert sand,
One single drop in oceans wide and deep—
Such is the import and significance
Of thy small life !   For if such globes are ruled
By the same laws this earthly world obeys,
If Death has entered other spheres than ours,
Where unknown myriads have been born and died,
As we must live and die and be forgot,
Then Man's imagination cannot grasp
Nor hold such totals of immensity !
Such things are hid, nor can we raise the veil ;
Such thoughts will rise, nor can we bid them stay,
But on quick wings they bear us unawares
To vaster problems than Man's mind can solve.

# ODE ON THE JUBILEE.

O QUEEN, the shadow of whose throne
    O'er half the world is cast ;
Thy people's glory is thine own,
    Their love for thee shall last.
Empress of Nations !   Wide and far
'Neath Southern Cross and Northern Star
    Thy sons are gath'ring fast
To pay thee homage who hast been
For half a century a Queen.

Behold how strong that throne may be
    Whose firm foundation stands,
Not on a despot's tyranny
    Nor strength of armèd bands,
But on a People's love and trust
Of her whose reign is good and just !
    Love, which the Ocean spans,
Hath bound our fealty to her throne,
Whose joys and sorrows are our own.

Not less a Queen we deemed her when
    The God of Love drew near ;
And she—a ruler over men—
    Bent down a listening ear ;
The robes of Empire could not hide
The beating heart of England's bride,
    Nor make her choice less dear ;
Her bridal wreath and bridal gems
Seemed more to her than diadems.

And now in zenith of her sway
  She sits upon the throne !
The glory of that bridal day
  Is gone : she reigns alone !
Ah ! Who shall read the thoughts which pass—
Like creeping shadows o'er the grass,
  When noon to eve has grown,—
Within her heart, and bring again
The Past with all its shadowy train !

Forget not, ye whose hearts are keen
  To pay the homage due,
Altho' an Empress and a Queen
  She is a *woman* too ;
And womanlike her thoughts will turn
From pomp and state she may not spurn
  But bears with calmness through,
To those she lost who cannot see
  The glory of her Jubilee.

God save her ! Hardly can be found
  A life more fair and pure ;
The love of millions guard her round
  And make her throne secure !
The power of noble womanhood
That bore the grief and chose the good
  Shall make her name endure.
A life and reign so nobly spent,
Will be her stateliest monument.

# ALONE.

The purple hills rise far behind,
  Before me spreads the plain,
The tall grass shakes beneath the wind
  Like surges on the main.
Thin mists have girt each low hill's crest,
  The hot sun swims in cloudless blue,
A mirage gathers in the West
  And trembles into view :
It gathers in the swimming haze,
  A silver lake of dazzling sheen,
Its waves are bright with dancing light
  And tender tints of blue and green.
A phantom sea, calm, limpid, wide,
  Sailed o'er by phantom ships !
Ah ! well I know that rippling tide
  Could never cool my lips.
My tongue is swollen in my mouth,
  My fevered lips are cracked and dry,
I hear the Spirit of the Drouth
  Whisper : " Thou soon shalt die ! "
The living shadow of a man,
  The living shadow of a horse,
Thro' heat and glare, in grim despair,
  We stagger on our unknown course.

Comrades, whose worth was sternly tried
  In hunger, thirst, and pain,
I ne'er shall see you at my side,
  Nor clasp your hands again !

Mine own weak hands scarce feel the reins,
  The hot wind burns my withered cheek,
So calm, so awful are the plains
  The silence seems to speak.
It almost seems to speak and say :
  " Those wronged by thee demand redress,
The hour draws nigh when thou shalt die,
  Alone within the wilderness ! "
Thro' shimmering grasses on I ride
  Across the yellow plain.
My comrades one by one have died,
  And I alone remain.
They sickened one by one, and died,
  The stout of heart, the strong of hand ;
Some lie upon the dark hillside,
  And some upon the sand.
Where never white man trod before,
  Thro' scrub, o'er plain, by mountain cleft,
We forced our way, until to-day
  This horse and I alone are left.


Down ! with a long and stagg'ring stride,
  The good horse falls to earth,
With staring eye and nostril wide—
  Small need to loose the girth !
There's hopeless anguish in his eyes,
  A rattling in his throat I hear,
" Water " is what he mutely cries,
  But not a drop is near.
He feebly sniffs my sunburnt hand,
  He feebly answers my caress,
Then gives one moan : I stand alone—
  Alone within the wilderness !

5

# MY LITTLE SWEETHEART.

My sweetheart is but five years old ;
  She has not learnt decorum yet ;
Her cheeks are pink ; her hair like gold ;
      Her eyes are violet.

And very sweet she seems to me—
  A little fairy full of grace,
With all her ringlets blowing free
      About her roguish face.

She pinches me, she pulls my hair,
  She steals my watch to hear it tick ;
I can't exactly tell you where
      She hid my hat and stick.

And oh ! she makes such " dreadful eyes "—
  This little angel without wings.
Do other angels in the skies
      Think of such wicked things ?

But sometimes she is very good
  And sits sedately on my lap
And hears me preach (as elders should)
      But doesn't care a rap.

And then she creeps up close to me,
  And lays her cheek against my own,
Whilst round my neck coquettishly
      Her tiny arms are thrown.

She tells me all her little cares ;
  Her childish griefs, and childish joys ;
How it was *she* who stole the pears !
      And how she hates the boys !

Ah ! little maid, at sweet seventeen
  You will not speak your heart to me ;
You will not kiss me *then*, I ween,
      Or sit upon my knee.

You will have scores of lovers *then*,
  And go to dances with your mother ;
And learn to play off gentlemen—
      The one against the other.

You will " sit out " in dusky nooks,
  And flirt, and smirk, and " take an ice,"
And think too much about your looks—
      And won't be half so nice.

You will have grown a skilful hand
  At drawing fish within your net ;
And few, I think, will long withstand
      Those eyes of violet.

I pray, dear, you may never feel
  The wrench which tears two lives apart,
The careless smiles which oft conceal
      The anguish of the heart ;

That Peace may fold thee in her wings,
  No thought arising, half confes't,
In spite of all that knowledge brings—
      That childhood's hours were best.

# THE RIVER OF DEATH.

I DREAMT that I stood by the River of Death,
And the breath of the wind was an icy breath ;
And the shades that hovered upon the bank
Heaved, and wavered, and rose, and sank.

And the shore was lit by a darkening light
Which shot thro' the Realms of Eternal Night ;
And the spell which hung on the heavy air
Was the spell of sorrow and dark despair.

Then I heard low wails, and sad echoings,
And sighs like the sweeping of heavy wings ;
But the tide rolled on, and its turbid wave,
Flowing for ever, no answer gave.

I strove to pierce thro' the distant gloom
Where the vague gigantic shadows loom ;
I strove to see to the farther shore,
But the rolling mists gathered more and more.

Then I stood on the brink, and I thought how strong,
Yet calm, that River had flowed along ;
Silent and mystical and sublime,
From the Springs of Sin on the verge of Time.

Passionless, darksome, yet ever on
It rolled thro' the ages past and gone ;
And it gathered the streams of Life as it went,
Till they one by one with its waters blent.

And I thought of the millions whose weary feet
Have stood on the brink where the shadows meet ;
Have stood in their doubt and their misery
By the River that flows to the Unknown Sea—

Of those who have heard, like a rolling drum,
The voice of the waters whisper " Come ! "
For only those who are called by Death
Can hear the words which that River saith.

Like the wash of the waves on a far-off shore
They hear the sound of the black flood's roar,
And deep in the stream where the tide runs strong
Interpret the words of its mystic song.

And I said, " O River, darksome and wide,
Is there room for me on thy silent tide ?
For my soul is filled with a fierce unrest,
And I fear not the chill of thine icy breast.

" The waters of Life are bitter, I ween,
Tho' the sun shines bright and the leaves are green
But peace comes not with the spring wind's breath,
For it lies far down in thy depths, O Death !—

" Where the sin and the sorrow and fierce unrest
Are buried deep 'neath the dark wave's crest,
And the longings wild and unsatisfied
Are swept away on thy rushing tide."

Still no answer came from the gath'ring gloom
Where the vague gigantic shadows loom,
But the tide rolled on, and its turbid wave,
Flowing for ever, no answer gave.

# LOVE AND AMBITION.

AMBITION, cased from head to heel
In armoured dress of glittering steel,
    Strode up a pathway narrow ;
Seeking for foes with warrior's joy,
He met a rosy little boy,
    Armed with a bow and arrow.
" Come, foolish child, and give," said he,
" That silly plaything up to me ;
    You'll harm yourself I fear."
" Nay," quoth the urchin with a grin,
" I see a chink your armour in,
    So do not come too near."
With loud contempt the giant laughed ;
Quick on the string Love placed a shaft,
    And bent his golden bow ;
The aim was swift, the aim was true.
Straight through the chink the arrow flew,
    And laid the giant low.
Dying, he raised his drooping head :
" I deemed no foe on earth," he said,
    " Could thus my breastplate pierce ;
Idiot to fail to recognize
That godlike form, those shining eyes,
    Which rule the universe."

# A MEDLEY.

EASTWARD in the skies of morning rosy tinges streak the
   gray,
Bars of crimson change to golden—glitt'ring heralds of
   the day,
Like a blood-red shield uprising swims the sun in palest
   blue,
Crowns the hills with crests of splendour, flashes on the
   trembling dew ;
Till the grass seems strewn with jewels, loosely strung,
   and red with dawn—
Nature's gems that gleam and quiver on the bosom of
   the Morn.
Far to Eastward, far to Northward, stretch the hills in
   purple chains,
Far to Southward, far to Westward, waves the grass on
   yellow plains ;
Fresh and blithely blow the breezes, drive the cloud,
   and move the lea
With the roll of grassy billows surging like a northern
   sea.
Ah ! what mem'ries stir within me as I ride thro' scenes
   like these,
Thro' the silence only broken by the voices of the
   breeze.
Voices of the rushing west wind chanting anthems weird
   and grand,
Mystic melodies of Nature that few hearts can understand.

I have loved the voice of Nature—loved the music of
    the breeze,
Sighing with a tender cadence thro' the branches of the
    trees ;
Loved the triumph of the Tempest blinding flash and
    deaf'ning roar,
When Heaven's batteries have opened, echoing from
    shore to shore.
Soft and tender is the fancy which thro' all my being
    thrills,
When the chequered lights and shadows play upon the
    purple hills ;
When the burning skies to westward fade to floods of
    amber light,
And the lemon tints of sunset melt into the dusks of night.
By the campfire in the silence when the light begins to
    wane,
Echoes of the dead, dead voices seem to fill the air again ;
When the tall stems of the gum trees stand like sheeted
    sentinels,
And the curlew's plaintive wailing sounds like weird
    funereal knells ;
Grander than the noblest poem, awful in its mystery,
Is a voice from mem'ry speaking when that voice has
    ceased to be.
I have sung the thoughts within me tho' the world may
    sneer and say :
In the vain pursuit of shadows he has cast his life away.
Never shall he merit honour who but works for praise
    alone ;
Never shall he gain a triumph who despairs when over-
    thrown ;
Never shall he wear the laurel who grows dumb when
    critics sting—
Whom the dread of censure silenced when the spirit
    bade him sing !

On the deep sea of existence like frail barks our lives
are blown,
Where the helmsman's hand is hidden and the harbour
is unknown.
He is best and he is noblest who has kept through good
and ill
Something of his purer nature, something of his childhood still.
But our souls grow stained and deadened, dark with
passion, sin, and care,
And we sow the seeds of folly, reap the harvest of
despair.
When amidst the roar of combat, thrust for thrust, and
stroke for stroke,
Sabres flash from blue to crimson, hissing through the
rolling smoke ;
When the bugle note is silent, and the rushing squadrons
reel,
Meeting in a shock like thunder, crash of harness, clash
of steel,
Gladly would I fall in battle fighting in the foremost
van,
For the sword of Sorrow pierceth deeper than the sword
of Man.
Idle thought ! To deem that dying thus could expiate
our sin,
That the soul could with the body perish in the battle's
din.
Death is but the gloomy portal to the realms of the
Unknown,
Where the laws that rule all Nature centre in one law
alone !
In the light beyond the Shadow, in that light beyond
the light,
Where the secrets of existence flash at last upon the
sight ;

In the deep beyond the distance, in the sphere beyond
  the spheres,
Truth has hid the golden keynote to the mysteries of
  years.
Ah ! I doubt not that hereafter we shall pass from change
  to change,
All the spirit growing finer, all the thought with wider
  range ;
On from region unto region where no mist our vision
  mars,
Till we see with perfect insight in some life beyond the
  stars.
There are deeper myst'ries hidden in the frailest flowers
  that blow
Than in all the lore of ages, all that greatest thinkers
  know.
Deem not tho' the flowers are withered that they will
  not come again ;
Winter sees them fade and perish, Spring will bring
  them with the rain.
Deem not tho' we pass in silence that we pass for ever-
  more—
Here we only grope in darkness wand'ring by an unknown shore.
Death will make us heirs of knowledge and unroll before
  the sight
Vistas of eternal splendour widening thro' the Infinite.

# FREDERICK III.

## Obiit June 15, 1888.

" His life was gentle ; and the elements
So mixed in him that Nature might stand up
And say to all the world, this was a man."
—Shakespeare.

On lordly terrace, and on palace wall,
  An awful silence crept ;
With noiseless footsteps up the columned hall
  An unseen presence swept—
God's angel, Azrael, whom men call Death,
Breathed on the monarch with his icy breath.

And as he passed, grasping his viewless brand,
  The shadow of his wings
Darkened the eagles of the Fatherland,
  From peasants unto kings
Rolled, like deep murmurs of a funeral drum
Thro' the wide world, a voice, " The end has come ! "

The world is German in this common grief ;
  She mourns the man alone.
Above the diadem, the laurel leaf,
  The sceptre, and the throne,
She sees the hero-soul ; and manhood's pride
Is nobler such a man has lived and died.

Look not upon the monarch but the man
Whom Death at length has freed.
Hero of nobler victories than Sedan !
The grandeur of whose creed
The world saw, and the world-wide whisper ran,
" Above the pride of kings, this was a man."

# A FEDERAL SONG.

THEY lay the stone whose eyes may never see
A Nation's turrets rise above the plain.
They sow the seed who may not reap the grain ;
  Futurity    .
Will bless that toil which wrought thro' stress and ·
 strain,
  Her Unity.

It yet shall be. Build on, and heed not scorn ;
Build fair and strong a nation's towering height ;
In massy grandeur weld her scattered might
  By schism torn.
After the darkness and the Dawn's gray light
  Cometh the Morn.

Build on ! Build on ! Hold with a nerve of steel,
Above all meaner pride and jealous hate,
That higher faith which makes a nation great.
  They rightly feel
Who take for the broad basement of the State
  The Common-weal.

Build on ! Build on ! Deep-pulsing thro' the land,
Thro' all this island-continent there stirs
A throb, a voice, she feels, and knows is hers,
  From strand to strand
A whisper stealing thro' the Dawn avers
  The hour at hand.

Build on ! Build on ! E'en as the restless blue
Circles her sleeping mountains, silence-bound,
Our hope, our faith, our love shall gird her round
    With fealty true,
Whilst from the old-world wrecks which strew the
    ground,
        We build anew.

## ORPHEUS TO EURYDICE.

THERE is no joy in Heaven if Love be not,
But, if we love, this Earth may yet be Heaven.
For what is Hell or Heaven but seed we sow,
Grown to maturity, within the soul ?
This is the law of Nature and the gods—
That each be free to act, yet by his acts
Achieve his misery or happiness.
Then choose we Heaven.  Let Duty temper love ;
For thro' its iron gate and flinty path
We reach the happy meadows, and, beyond,
The Highest Good ; and, if that path be rough,
Deep-shadowed, dreary, 'tis not all so dark
But Love can light it ; for the soul that grasps
Love only, spurning duty, knows not Love,
But passion, which consumes the soul and leaves
A Hell within it.  Therefore, O my Love,
Choose we the better part.  Let passion be ;
And, if our lot be lowly, and our lives
The common round of petty care and toil,
Who is there that would choose voluptuous ease,
Feeling his manhood in him ; and his heart
Strong to resist the buffets of the world,
The long stern struggle, and the frequent fall ?
For in the toil and in the strife alone
We find our strength, until at last we stand
High on Olympus, even as the gods.
There shall we gaze back at the years and know

'Twas for the best.   Ah !   in a world like ours
There is no obstacle but falls before
The strength of an indomitable will
Linked to a love like thine.   Come thou to me.
My soul is thine.   Thou art my destiny.
The gods have whispered it.   Thro' all this Life
Thy soul and mine are wedded, and beyond,
Thro' Death, to the Hereafter, Love shall lead
And we shall follow.   It is Destiny.
No change can alter and no power avert
The Unseen Hand that gathers where it will
Two lives, and welds them in one living love.

# ODE ON THE AUSTRALIAN CENTENARY.

GIRT with the wreathing mists
And shadows of the night,
Dark-robed, Australia lay
And waited for the light ;
And heard the night wind whisper soft and clear :
"Land of the Southern Cross, the Dawn is near !
The Dawn is near ! "

Soft in the Eastern skies,
Flushing the summer sea,
She saw her morning rise—
The morn of Liberty.
Then sang the wind across the ocean's foam :
"Land of the Southern Cross, the Dawn has come,
The Dawn has come ! "

Blest with God's grace divine,
Queen of the Southern Sea !
Bright shall thy glory shine,
Great shall thy future be.
Our hope, our faith, our love, on Him we cast.
"Land of the Southern Cross, the Dawn is past,
The Dawn is past ! "

Past with its quivering rays—
Forecasts of things to be !
Past to the riper days
Of larger Liberty !
Then sing, ye summer seas that guard our home :
"Behold ! The Dawn is past ! The Day has come,
The Day has come ! "

# MARY MAGDALENE.

A CHILD of sin and crowned with shame
Unto the Master's feet she came ;
From shapely head to ankle bare
Fell the broad ripples of her hair ;
And for a soft and radiant dress
She wore her loveliness.

A perfect form, a faultless face,
Fairer than sculptor's art could trace ;
Ripe as the full rose in its prime
Ere yet it feels the touch of Time ;
But now with suppliant eyes she stood—
The type of fallen womanhood.

Meekly she stood, whose wanton pride
Had flung all purity aside ;
Whose lips had tasted poisonous wine—
The deadly vintage of that vine
Whose green and comely branches bear
The fruit of Passion and Despair.

Silent she stood, with weary feet,
And heart whose joy had ceased to beat ;
For all the charms that Pleasure brought
Calmed not the maddening voice of thought,
The fierce unrest, the cruel pain,
Of one who hopes—and hopes in vain.

The sunshine wrapt her in its fold
And tinged her burnished hair with gold ;
On silken lashes, darkly hung,
The beaded tear-drops, trembling, clung ;
She seemed more fair in her despair
Than ever in the days that were.

No gift she brought—yet one complete—
Who washed with tears the Master's feet.
She gave a gem of priceless worth
Above the jewels of the Earth ;
For, with true faith, and eyes with sorrow dim,
She gave her heart to Him.

# THE BAR IMMUTABLE.

IN the long lingering hours when Earth lies hid
In robes of darkness, and the night has come
To reign alone in calm sweet majesty,
When Sleep on aërial wing has fled away
And given no solace to the throbbing brain,
Oft have I trod the corridors of Thought
And watched, as from the tombs of Memory
The ghosts of long dead years arise and pass
In slow procession—erstwhile, Kings of Time,
But now dethroned, discrowned, and sceptreless ;
Shrouded in silence and in mystery.
Glide on, ye Phantom Monarchs of the Past,
In solemn grandeur !  From the sepulchres
That fringe the burial ground of centuries
Gray rolling clouds and misty damps arise
Wherein vivific currents flash and dart ;
As meteors crossing the ethereal blue
At dazzling speed—for one swift instant crown
The brow of night with splendid aureole ;
So flashes Memory's lightning thro' the Past
Whitening the shadows, 'till all luminous
The vista stretches, and the eye discerns
The half-forgotten scenes, the moving throng
Of old familiar faces : All that *was*
But nevermore again on Earth *shall be.*
With solemn steps I pace the paths I trod
In youth's sweet spring, when inexperienced thought

Pictured the Future as a pleasant dream
And gilded life with rich deceptive hue ;
I hear again soft and reverberant
The echoes of dead voices in the air ;
And all the good and evil of long years
Is mirrored in the glass of Retrospect.
But what avails it, if we ever thus
Stand gazing down the misty aisles of thought
And robe our lives with Mem'ry's fantasies ?
Time's rushing flood has reached and passed them by,
And still sweeps on.   For who and what can stand
Before the force of that resistless flood ?
All, all, go down before it.   Beauty, Age,
The golden dreams of Youth, fair Fancy's halls,
The airy castles proud Ambition built,
Swept at its touch to cold Oblivion's shore.
The mystery of Life hangs o'er my soul
In weighted horror.   For what shall we gain
If by long arduous pilgrimage we reach
The highest pinnacles of human thought ?
'Tis but the limit which our faculties
May touch but not exceed : The key of Death
Alone can ope the gates of the Unseen.

.      .      .      .      .      .      .

A higher gift than reason must be ours
Ere we can comprehend that germ of life
Which permeates Nature, understand the Pow'r
That rules ethereal principalities,
Makes chaos worlds, conceives eternities.
Rough lies the path, dim-lighted, and beyond—
The dark Unknown : That bar immutable,
At which our thoughts in weak confusion pause
And beat their wings against the gates of Heaven.

# RETROSPECTION.

ALONE she stood, with careless grace,
　Like one whose thoughts were far away :
Upon her tender girlish face
　I watched the lights and shadows play ;
I watched the fringes of her eyes
　Sweep her soft cheek ; and overhead
From the calm heights of summer skies,
　Thro' leafy boughs the sunbeams spread ;
Nor could I judge which seemed most fair,
The sunshine or her golden hair.

Around her feet the violets grew ;
　Above her head the woodland birds
Made music in a key so true,
　I would not change it into words.
'Twas Nature's song in Nature's scene,
　And she was Nature's fairest flower ;
And that which *is* and might have been
　Were all unthought of in that hour.
I had not learnt, I did not guess,
How joy can turn to bitterness.

The Past is gone.　The rolling years
　Have brought their pleasures and their pain ;
And change, and manhood's hopes and fears,
　Will chase such phantoms from the brain.

Our lives in different grooves are cast,
And she has other cares to bear ;
The misty curtain of the past
Divides us from the days that were.
Yet through the haze I often see
That face which once was all to me.


It may be that the influence
Of those old days hangs round me still ;
It may be that a finer sense
Will guard the hand from deeds of ill ;
It may be that, if aught of good
My life has shown or tried to show,
If aught of suffering was withstood
With seeming patience, all I owe
To her I loved, whose memory brings
The thoughts of nobler purer things.


Scoff not at youth.  In youth alone
Our thoughts are pure, our hearts are true ;
For then we have not learnt to own
How vain the phantoms we pursue.
And what is life, and what is man,
Without that freshness of the heart
Which once was ours, but never can
Return when youth and faith depart ?
Time gives us much, but who will say—
*As much* as all it takes away.

# IN THE BIG WARD.

A WAN white cheek on the pillow lying ;
  A fevered gleam in the dark brown eye ;
Not twelve years old—and the boy is dying
  Inch by inch as the days roll by !

Inch by inch as the days are fleeting
  The young life drifts where its pain shall cease,
Where the weary heart shall stay its beating,
  And the soul shall sleep 'neath the wings of Peace.

In the white-washed ward there are faces dreary,
  Low moans of anguish and laboured breath ;
But none so patient and yet so weary
  As the child who lies there waiting for death.

Men scorn thee, Death, amidst squadrons crashing,
  When the red steel leaps in the strong right hand ;
Men hold it but gain when sabres are flashing
  To die for their faith and their Fatherland.

Men face thee, Death, with a nerve unshaken,
  On the deadly breach in the fortress wall ;
But bravest he who by hope forsaken
  Endures like the child in this white-washed hall.

Ah ! Why must the children suffer and languish,
  And wince and quiver beneath thy thong ?
Why crush, O Death, with thy terrible anguish
  The pure young lives that have done no wrong ?

'Tis hard to know that the strong are dying,
Yet manhood and death may be reconciled ;
But O 'tis harder to hear the sighing,
And watch the pangs, of a helpless child !

Friend ! Who knows in the dim hereafter
If shall be meted to him again
For tears and anguish, sweet love and laughter,
A cycle of joy for a season of pain ?

But this we know—that the curse primeval,
Which strikes alike at the weak and strong,
Spares not the children, who did no evil,
But stays their laughter and stills their song.

# IN MEMORIAM.

(Viola, a talented contributor to *The Queenslander*, was lately drowned at sea.)

Sweet is the sleep of Death that brings
  Release from life, relief from pain ;
Where Trouble's joyless echoings
  Can never reach the ear again ;
But the white wings of Peace are spread
Like Angel's pinions overhead.

Sleep on ! where the dark billows roll
  And the sea-breezes whisper low ;
Sleep on ! Beyond our weak control
  A deeper wisdom wills it so ;
What men call Death is but the shadowy night
Which links the Finite with the Infinite.

Deep be thy sleep, beyond all pain ;
  Nor doubt that in the Spheres above
The majesty of Death shall wane
  Beside the majesty of Love.
Tho' Death may pluck the purest flowers and best,
'Tis but that God may fold them closer to His breast.

# DEATH.

O DEATH, and must thy marble hand
  Be laid upon each human heart ?
Can none dispute thy dread command,
  All-powerful tyrant that thou art ?
Seeming afar, but ever near—
  A sword suspended overhead,
How slight the causes can appear
  Which hurl the sword and part the thread !
And often in the early spring,
  When hope is young and life is sweet,
Is seen the shadow of thy wing,
  Is heard the echo of thy feet.
And oft thou comest unawares,
  When life is in its summer prime,
Turning our pleasures into cares
  And summer into winter time ;
Seeming afar, but ever near—
  So when at length our parting breath
We yield Thee—in another sphere
  Thou giv'st us Life, Almighty Death.

# THREE YEARS AGO.

Not many years have passed away
  Since last I saw that gentle face ;
    Not many years !
To those whose hearts are light and gay
  The time of such a little space
    Swift disappears.
But those few years have been to me
A weary blank eternity.


Three years ago ! I knew you then,
  You were the fairest of the fair ;
    Three years ago !
Your beauty stirred the hearts of men,
  They said none could with yours compare ;
    I loved you so,
I felt with pride my bosom swell
To hear her praised I loved so well.


Where beauties grew like comely flowers,
  Your stately grace outshone them all,
    Like some sweet rose
Which from the sheltering leafy bowers
  Has climbed the garden wall,
    And lovelier grows ;
Blooms Queen amongst the roses there,
Sweet like her sisters, but more fair.

You thought it was a boyish dream
  That future years would drive away ;
    Three years have past.
That years like centuries can seem,
  That weeks seems years, an hour a day,
    I know at last ;
But still my " boyish dream " remains,
Still in my heart thine image reigns.

" Come what come may ! " I know that now
  For ever thou art lost to me,
    In three short years.
To Fate's relentless law I bow,
  And wish all happiness to thee,
    Till Death appears
With lightning stride or footstep slow ;
I love you as " Three Years Ago."

# TO NINA.

Nina, if a heart be true
  Whatsoever it endures,
Faithful as the skies are blue,
  Nina, then that heart is yours.
If I sought a friend to find
  (When my friends were far and few)
Loving, pitiful, and kind,
  Nina, I should turn to you.

Think not, tho' the Ocean wide,
  Restless, seething, rolls between,
Those upon the farther side
  Your devotion have not seen.
Think not tho' Pacific's tide
  Keeps you hidden from our view
That we, as the seasons glide,
  Think less lovingly of you.

You have proved your love to be
  No mere empty hollow form
But a stout old oaken tree
  Which can weather any storm.
And, as years roll on, its root
  Shall but gain a firmer hold.
Friendships like the juice of fruit
  But grow mellow when they're old.

And tho' now Australia's sky
  Forms our starry canopy,
Yet our thoughts will often fly
  To our home beyond the sea.
In a race the winning steed
  Boldly all the fences clears,
So our thoughts like coursers speed
  And outstrip the crawling years.

And when Time has done his worst,
  And our heads are old and gray,
Some of us our chains have burst,
  And those left care not to stay ;
When a mound and hollow urn
  Tells the world we are no more,
Friendship's torch will brighter burn,
  Nina, on another shore !

# LINES ON THE DEATH OF LONGFELLOW.[1]

THE singer mute, the lyre unstrung,
Dust—first from off earth's bosom sprung—
 To earth return !
Yet a great quenchless torch of song,
Lit by no feeble hand, shall strong
 For ever burn.

Its light shall shine from strand to strand,
And, blazing o'er that Western land,
 The ocean span ;
And great posterity shall read
The tenets of a Christ-like creed—
 Goodwill to man.

And though within the grave they lay
An earthly tenement of clay,
 And mourn thy loss,
Thou standest by thy Master's side
Who for thy sake was crucified
 Upon the cross.

Far truer honour than the wreath
Of sadly coloured laurel leaf,
 Which decks thy tomb,
Was the great throb of sympathy
For all those near and dear to thee,
 In this—their gloom.

[1] The poet died on the 27th of February, 1882.

# CHRISTMAS.

ONCE more breaks the joyous morning !
    Christmas Day is here !
Once more see the welcome dawning
    Of a glad New Year !
Once more gather round the entrance
    Of the church's door,
Rich and poor, and proud and lowly,
Strong and weak, the meek, the holy ;
Gathered there to worship Him whom heaven and earth
    adore.

Happy faces !  Bright reflections
    Of the hearts within ;
Faces showing stern corrections
    For some former sin ;
Faces aged, and worn, and weary ;
    Faces young and fair,
Faces beautiful from sorrow,
Faces careless of the morrow,
Faces gloomy, sad, and thoughtful,
    All are there.

# CHRISTMAS.

WITH sweet memories, kindly faces
 Thronging joyous in his train ;
Thro' the world Old Christmas paces,
 Binds us with a golden chain,
Chains of Love and bonds of Friendship, fetters firm yet
 light to bear,
And before his face the shadows fade and vanish into air.


 Yet amidst our Christmas gladness
  Comes a feeling deep and wide,
 Runs a vein of tender sadness
  Like some zephyr o'er the tide,
As we speak with softened voices and a secret cruel pain
Of those hearts we loved, whom Christmas nevermore will
 greet again.


 Not for long and not for ever
  Is our sojourn here below ;
 Sorrows throng and Death will sever
  Hearts which no dissensions know ;
Yet while we remember sadly those we ne'er shall see
 again
Let us keep a hearty greeting for the friends who still
 remain.

Then with gentle tact, not wrongly,
Put aside the vacant chair,
Not because we feel less strongly,
That the loved one is not there ;
But because Life lies before us and we all must bear our
load,
And we needs must cheer each other for we climb a
rugged road.


Shall we vex our dear ones living
By our mem'ries of the Dead ?
Shall we sadden this thanksgiving
By the fruitless tears we shed ?
If the spirit be Eternal, Death and Sorrow, what are they
But the gates unbarred which open upwards to the larger
Day ?

# THE UNKNOWN LAND.

CHRISTMAS again !  With a solemn tread
  Comes the Monarch old and gray,
To join the years that are gone and dead,
  The hopes that have passed away ;
And with mournful eyes I watched him stand
On the shadowy verge of that Unknown Land.

His brow was not crowned with the silver frost,
  He wore not his robe of snow ;
His wreaths of holly-tree were lost,
  And his wand of mistletoe ;
But in emerald robes of leaf and moss
He stood 'neath the light of the Southern Cross.

And heavy the burden the old man bore
  On his shoulders wide and vast,
To the tomb of the years that have gone before,
To the silent shades of Oblivion's shore,
  To the Sepulchre of the Past ;
The thought, the faith, the hope, the fear,
Of millions were laid on the dying year.

And I said : " Old man, with the beard of snow,
  And the dim and failing eyes,
Where are the friends of long ago,
Who have learnt the secret we do not know ;
  And shall they yet arise
To greet us again with outstretched hand
On the shadowy shores of that Unknown Land ? "

Then in solemn tones the seer replied :
"All things must pass away ;
But those who strive to stem the tide,
Who bear in labour side by side
   The burden of the day,
Shall grasp again on that silent shore
The hands of those who have gone before."

He was gone, but I did not see him go
   In his green and leafy dress ;
For I sat and thought of the care and woe
In many a home that I used to know ;
   And the joy and happiness
Which Death removes with unsparing hand,
But which God restores in that Unknown Land.

# TO BRENDA SLEEPING.

( FROM " LORAINE," AN UNPUBLISHED POEM.)

O PEACE !   Kiss her eyes with thy wings, let her
  slumbers be sweet
  And  calm 'neath the shadow  of  pinions majestic and
  still,
With dreams like the music of waters in rhythmical beat,
  And guard her for ever from sorrow and shield her from
  ill ;

From the taint of my love, from the passion and quenchless unrest,
  The storm of despair which is rising tumultuous and
  fierce !
O Peace, if thy wings have for ever forsaken my breast,
  Fold them closer around her like shields which no
  sorrow can pierce !

# LANCELOT.

I SEE thro' mists of dark despair,
  Her stately form arise ;
The glimmer of her golden hair
  The radiance of her eyes.
Mercy is thine, Immortal Powers !
  O make her soul, beyond the skies,
Pure as the amaranthine flowers
  That bloom in Paradise.
*My* soul conceived the deadly sin,
  And on *my* soul let vengeance fall.
I bow the knee to Heaven's decree—
  But in Thy love forgive her all.


Too late ! Too late ! for hope or prayer !
  My eyes grow glazed and weak,
I stagger in the blinding glare,
  Too faint at last to speak ;
My soul is sick and dark within ;
  A voice is pealing thro' the air :
" Who sow the deadly seeds of sin
  Shall only reap despair."
And, stricken by that awful voice,
  I sink upon the burning sod ;
And in the Fate for which I wait,
  I recognize the hand of God.

# LOVE AND FAME.

Night shook o'er Earth her raven locks,
  Black clouds had curtained all the sky ;
And with long sighs and bursting shocks,
  The restless winds went roaring by.

A sculptor sat in loose attire,
  With dreamy eyes fixed on the blaze ;
Within the glowing heart of fire
  He saw the scenes of other days.

In many a line from wall to wall
  The blocks of milk-white marble stood ;
Cupids, and stalwart knights and tall,
  And types of lovely womanhood.

Pale was his face, and thin with care—
  None sought to buy his works of Art ;
The darkness of a grim despair
  Was spreading slowly o'er his heart.

" Alas ! " he sighed, " no man may be
  A prophet in his native land ;
Or Fate has laid her curse on me,
  And marred the cunning of my hand.

" And she I love says ' Love is dead,'
  And laughs to scorn my dreams of Fame ;
The light of other days has fled,
  And left me only care and shame.

" I cannot carve upon the stone
    The vision that I see in air—
The face of her I love alone,
    The face that haunts me everywhere.

Then in his ear a whisp'ring voice
    Spake softly : " Carve upon the stone
The angel vision of thy choice—
    The face of her thou lov'st alone.

" Carve thou Love's Angel, sweet and fair,
    With deathless face and wings outspread,
The Power that rules us everywhere ;
    And she will say—' Love is not dead.' "

Then from his seat the sculptor rose ;
    The fadeless light of genius shone
Upon his brow.   With skilful blows
    He wrought upon the milk-white stone.

And slowly from the stone there grew
    The outlines, mystical and grand ;
And, tho' unseen to mortal view,
    An angel sped the sculptor's hand.

Long hours he wrought with steadfast face
    Till the dim grays ot morn flushed clear ;
Noon passed, and twilight grew apace,
    And Night's dark pinions hovered near.

And still he wrought, and when the Dawn
    Crowned the blue hills with roseate light,
Bathed in the glory of the morn—
    Love's Angel shone in spotless white,

With deathless face, and wings outspread ;
  And smiling, from the milk-white stone,
Her face who said that Love was dead—
  The face of her he loved alone,

But made divine.  He gazed, and knew
  The vision he had seen in air ;
Then on the ground his chisel threw,
  And slept beside the Angel there,

Slept long and sound—a dreamless sleep—
  The sleep of Death.  And she who said
" Love is no more " crept there to weep,
  " O my true love, Love is not dead."

      .    .    .    .    .    .

Night shook o'er Earth her sable locks ;
  Black clouds had curtained all the sky,
And with long sighs and bursting shocks
  The restless winds went roaring by.

The wild winds sang : " When Death shall free
  The throbbing brain, the toiling hand,
Then, *only then*, a man may be
  A prophet in his native land."

# THE SINGER.

SHE sang of Hope, of happy days,
  Of glorious spring and summer's prime ;
Softer than old-time minstrels' lays
  Uprose that melody sublime.

She sang of Faith, of firm resolve,
  Of strong unwavering constancy ;
To trust and live till death should solve
  The problem of life's mystery.

She sang of Death—that sceptre grim—
  Of pain, and age, and faltering gait ;
Of eyes once bright, now faint and dim ;
  Of hearths and homes made desolate.

She sang of Love ; and as she sang
  Her colour came and went again ;
No words can tell how clearly rang
  The cadence of that sweet refrain.

She sang no more ; for on that night
  There came a shadow and a gloom
Which hid the singer from our sight,
  And hung around a darkened room.

And now she sings where angels sing
  A nobler song in spheres above ;
Where Death no more can enter in,
  And Hope and Faith are lost in Love.

But from the echoes of the past
   Her voice comes ringing back again,
To tell the hearts who knew her last
   That Hope and Faith and Love remain.

# DISCONTENT.

Does the daily round seem dreary ?
Does the path of life seem rough ?
Do we find our steps grow weary,
   Thinking we have toiled enough ?
      In the west
Looms the stormy cloudy weather
With no shining silver lining,
Soul and body tire together ;
   All we feel—a yearning pining
      But for rest.
Cease my soul this sinful sighing ;
   Is thy path to be all roses ?
Prizes won without the trying ?
   Pleasures where no cross opposes
      What you will ?
Is another's lot so sunny
   That thou need'st must thus repine
Is the corn and oil and honey
   To be nobody's but thine ?
      Peace !   Be still !
'Tis the path we all must follow,
   'Tis the common destiny ;
Pleasure's prizes are but hollow,
   Sweet delusive mockery.
      Time doth teach

Life is meant to be not pleasures,
    Not all dull laborious toil,
But two happy blended measures
    Acting as a counterfoil
        Each to each.
There are stars whose rays have never
    Reached this world of sin and sorrow ;
Travelling onward, travelling ever,
    Still their advent is to-morrow,
        Still to-morrow !
Through immeasurable spaces,
    Through the voids all uncreated,
Past the high eternal places,
    Still their advent must be dated,
        " Still to-morrow."
Like the starlight which is roaming
    Earthwards, though without our view,
Perhaps to-morrow in life's gloaming
    Some glad change may come for you—
        As the ray,
Long deferred and long expected,
    Seems a brighter hue to borrow
From the hopes of years reflected
    In its advent—not " to-morrow,"
        But " to-day."
There are silent depths of ocean
    Which no sounding line can measure,
Airy regions where the motion
    Of the kingly eagle's pinions
        Is unknown.
The vast secrets which'are hidden,
    Like some deeply buried treasure,
All shall solve when they are bidden,
    To death's drearisome dominions—
        But alone !

There are secret workings hidden,
  In the dull monotony ;
Though foreknowledge is forbidden,
  Veiled from human scrutiny.
          Leave to One
Who can comprehend our yearnings—
  Human weakness, doubt, and sorrow—
All thy passionate heart-burnings :
  He will not forget thy morrow
          When thy work is done.

# VÂLÈ.

WITHIN my soul I hear the strain—
 The cadence of a song which tells
That Life is mingled joy and pain,
 And made of greetings and farewells.
Ever the currents of Life's tide
 Flow thro' the channels Fate has made
O'er plain, by rugged mountain-side,
 And now in sunshine, now in shade.
I pray the Unseen Hand may steer
 Your course through life with face serene,
With deeper joys from year to year,
 Where Care's dark shadows are not seen.
If Northern skies should seem bereft
 Of that which makes the Southern fair,
Our sun has kissed your eyes and left
 Its rays of softened glory there.
So do not say you fear to dwell
 Where skies are grey and winds are chill
The radiance of a sunnier clime
 Will linger round your presence still.
And when through other scenes you roam
 And other voices greet your ear,
Your thoughts at times may wander home
 To dwell with some who miss you here ;
*Then* if my " rude untutored lines "
 By chance offend not, let them be
As links within a chain which binds
 My homage to your memory.

Life is a maze where paths entwine
  But to diverge as Fortune tends
Until we pass that trembling line
  Where Love begins and Friendship ends.
And still within my soul I hear
  That song's sweet melancholy swell,
And all that I will whisper, dear,
  Is simply greeting and—Farewell !

# AUSTRALIA MILITANT.

(WRITTEN ON THE DEPARTURE OF THE AUSTRALIAN
TROOPS FOR THE SOUDAN.)

BLOW soft, ye southern breezes, blow ! For see
How bright the star which guards our destiny
          Sheds its soft ray !
Sail on, ye warriors, on your northward course,
And bear the banner of the Southern Cross
          Far in the fray
Where the old war-worn standard waves, and dare—
Beside those glorious folds—to plant it there !

When furious and fast the battel runs,
Australia's eyes will watch her soldier sons ;
          When through the haze
Of battle clouds the dusky hordes appear,
Australia's sons will hold her honour dear.
          Should glory's rays
Shine where the southern banners proudly wave,
Then not in vain her chivalry she gave !

When the swift-shooting spear and hissing ball
Sing through the thinning ranks, and comrades fall ;
          When like the blast
Bursts the wild charge upon the square again—
Bursts like a flood the human hurricane ;
          Then stern and fast
In the dread breach may Young Australia stand,
Firm as the mountains of her native land !

# THE SHEPHERD'S LAST SLEEP.

In the old log hut the shepherd lay,
  His fevered cheek by the hot wind fanned ;
And he dreamt of the dear ones far away,
  And the fields and the flowers of his native land.

And o'er his face crept a tender smile
  As he dreamt of one who was dearer still,
And the stately home in his native isle.
  Ah ! if dreams could only their vows fulfil !

To the old log hut by the lonely creek
  With naked sword came the Angel of Death ;
Pale grew the sleeper's hectic cheek
  As he felt the touch of that icy breath.

In the lonely bush in a far-off land,
  Where the wattles bloom and the brigalows wave ;
Laid to his rest by a stranger's hand,
  The exile sleeps in his nameless grave.

# SUBMISSION.

Each thinks no trial harder than his own ;
   Each thinks his cross the heaviest is to bear ;
There are no hearts where sorrow is unknown,
   And care is everywhere.
There is no sweet without some bitter sting—
   No rose without a thorn ;
The man who shall not know what anguish is,
   Is yet unborn.
Yet some there be who murmur at their lot,
   And waste their strength in striving to be free ;
Some who, impatient, crave they know not what,
   And brood in vain o'er what can never be.
And some there be who round their fetters twine
   A garland of fresh leaves and roses fair—
Brave hearts, who struggle on and ne'er repine,
   And gladness carry with them everywhere.
Oh, restless, seething mass !—Humanity !
   Borne down, yet struggling on in mute despair !
There is no cross which man on earth hath borne
   Which man still cannot bear.

# MARION RAYNE.

THE roses have climbed up the garden wall,
But one hangs highest above them all—
The sweet Queen-Rose on her slender stem,
With the morning dew for a diadem ;
As her delicate leaves to the sun she spreads
The roses beneath her must hang their heads,
   Sweet Marion Rayne !

The lilies that float on the still lagoon
Are pale as the rays of the crescent moon,
And I strove to judge, with a sweet despair,
Which was the fairest that floated there ;
An equal homage I paid to each,
Till I spied one floating beyond my reach—
   Sweet Marion Rayne !

The violets lie thick in their modest bed,
And sweet on the air is the scent they shed ;
I have plucked the flowers that you love the best
To lie on the heaven of your tender breast ;
But the sweetest flower in the tiny sheaf
I found concealed 'neath a shady leaf,
   Fair Marion Rayne !

It is high to reach to the red red rose ;
The water looks deep where the lily grows ;

But tell me, dear, may the lily rare,
Or the rose, be plucked if a heart can dare ?
Must the fairest flower that Nature made
Bloom on alone till her beauties fade,
            Sweet Marion Rayne ?


Is it pride that shines in your deep dark eyes,
And makes your soft bosom sink and rise ?
Is it love or pride that has blanched your cheek—
That trembles on lips which refuse to speak ?
And why is your face so cold and set ?
Is true love hid like the violet,
            Sweet Marion Rayne ?

# SAILING.

AH !   How freshly blew the breezes
   As they bore us from the shore !
All that pleasure's senses pleases
   Lingers round those days of yore.
      As our snow-white lateen sail
   Bellied out before the wind,
And our boat beneath it reeling
Onward rushed until 'twas heeling
         Almost o'er ;
   And we flew before the gale
   And the white waves roared behind.

When you raised your voice to sing
   In a key so strong and true,
E'en the sea-birds on the wing
   Seemed to pause and list to you.
      Deep the meaning of your song
   Rolled into mine inmost soul ;
All the ocean air was ringing
With the sweetness of your singing,
      And my secret kept so long
   Burst at last from my control.

# YOU AND I.

(SONG FROM "LORAINE," AN UNPUBLISHED POEM.)

WE met, you and I, in the morning fair
  When the sun shone bright and the skies were blue.
No shadow of sorrow, no thought of care
Had chilled the breath of the summer air,
  And my soul went out to you—
Went out with a fierce and passionate beat,
Went out with a fervent and quivering heat,
  A love that was tender and true.

We parted, Love, in the twilight grey,
  When the mists had gathered over the sea.
And I knew that the Dawn of another day,
The sheen on the sea, and the strong sun's ray,
  Could bring no happiness back to me.
Ah ! What is there left but grief and pain
For the heart that loves—and loves in vain !

But I pray in my grief that thy life may be
  Crowned with the joy of a shadowless calm.
And my heart will follow thee over the sea
For my soul is linked with thy destiny
  To guard from sorrow and shield from harm,
  Tho' my love is nothing to thee.
Tho' the love that I crave for thou canst not give—
  And I ask for nought or thy whole heart's store—
The love that I bear thee will blossom and live
  When my soul has passed to the Unknown Shore ;
The love that I bear thee will blossom and live
  When Time and Sorrow shall be no more.

# THE CHURCHYARD OF THE SEA.

FULL many a fathom buried deep
  In silent rest they lie ;
In Ocean's coral caves they sleep
  To 'wait eternity—
Whose lives—the Brave—the True—the Free—
Were swallowed in the angry sea ;
Who now have found a calmer rest
  In Ocean's breast.

'Midst shattered wrecks, 'midst treasure vast,
The sunken wealth of ages past,
  They slumber side by side ;
Captains and tars before the mast,
  The husband and the bride ;
The brother bold, the sister dear,
The hoary sage, the buccaneer,
  The meek, the sons of Pride :
Death knows of no distinctions here
  Beneath the rolling tide !

And when our time shall come to learn
  O grave ! thy mystery,
Where can our bones find fitter urn
  Than in thy depths, O Sea ?
To lie beneath the restless wave
Far in some hidden ocean cave
With these—the Free—the True—the Brave—
  Until eternity ;
And let the tranquil voiceless deep
  Our secrets keep.

# LOVE'S AMBUSH.

When first the little God of Love,
Descending from the skies above,
Alit on earth, he closed his wings
And gazed around on earthly things ;
Then sought with eagerness to find
A dwelling suited to his mind.
Full long he sought with cheerless face,
Nor found the wished-for resting-place ;
Till, almost sinking with despair ;
He spied a woman, young and fair.
Quick, with a cry of glad surprise,
Love ran and hid in woman's eyes ;
Ambushed in those sweet eyes he lay,
And shot his arrows every way ;
Of many a *spark* his target made,
On many a heart his arrows played ;
So strong his bow, so true his aim,
He changed each *spark* into a *flame ;*
But flames to fiercer flames soon turned
And while the furnace brightly burned,
The wicked imp enjoyed the fun
And laughed to think what he had done.
My friend, if you'd be good and wise,
Gaze not too long in woman's eyes.
But if you needs must gaze—Beware !
*The God of Love may still be there !*

# LOVE'S CONQUEST.

I SEE them gather for the fight
Beneath the castle wall ;
Full many a bold and doughty knight
Who shall, before the evening's light,
Within th' arena fall ;
But now each in his pride and might
Awaits the bugle call.

Each knight is in full armour dressed,
With glittering lance in hand ;
Brightly on breastplate, helm, and crest,
The golden rays of morning rest ;
And, by ambition fanned,
High beats within each warrior's breast
The hope of Edith's hand.

Each pawing war-steed shakes his mane,
Impatient of delay,
And fretted by the curbing rein,
Curvets, and paws the earth again,
And snorts to join the fray ;
Then, finding all his efforts vain,
Yields to his rider's sway.

High o'er the lists the royal stand
Its lofty front uprears :
There sits the monarch of the land,
Bravest of all that martial band,
Surrounded by his peers ;
And his the warlike mind that planned
That mustering of spears.

And on that serried mass of mail-clad men
  From balcony above
A galaxy of beauty, which no pen
  Could draw save that of Love,
Looked down with glance so arch and bright and free
That Love his pen had dropped in ecstasy.


Fairer than all the daughters of the court,
  Who all were young and fair,
Like some pale lily freshly culled, and brought
Amidst the roses, and yet losing nought
  Of her pure glory there
(Nay, rather there her matchless beauty shone
The lovelier by the sweet comparison),
  Sits Editha the fair.


All round her head her wavy golden hair
  Clusters, then like some sea
Falls rippling o'er her shoulders, thick and fair,
  Until it gains her knee ;
Her eyebrows black as jet : a silken fringe
Of kindred hue shadows each violet eye,
Where burns a light so queenly, pure, and true,
  That of that company
Of knights and vassals—all that courtly train—
Not one but would have died to save her pain.


Her face is oval, and her ruby lips
  Half-parted—not in scorn—
Like two twin rosebuds which the queen bee sips
  Upon some dewy morn,
Reveal, like ocean pearls, her teeth of snow ;
Her nose one straight fine line joined to a forehead low
But wide ; her throat, an ivory column rose below :
  The clinging drapery worn

Displays the soft curves of her splendid form—
Model for Venus ; born to take by storm.
But, ever and anon, there came and went
    Upon her cheek a hue
Which rivalled damask, till its power was spent.


    Then once again there grew
A deadly pallor over all her face,
Her sweet eyes roamed o'er all that peopled space,
As if in search of one whose knightly place
    Was vacant ; and it threw
A cruel anguish in those tender orbs,
A sickening dread, which all things else absorbs.


But hark ! the first of the alarms
    The heralds quickly sound,
And chargers prance, and knights adjust their arms
    O'er all the tourney ground ;
And beauties forward lean, and to their charms
Are added sparkling eye and rosier cheek ;
But whiter grew one cheek, and her heart's qualms
    No soothing solace found ;
But pale, betwixt anxiety and dread ;
She sat like one whose only hope has fled.


Hark ! List again ! The second trumpet sounds
    Its warning clear and shrill ;
Then rises, 'midst that sheen of spears and shields,
The Great Knight—victor in a hundred fields,
And all around with gathering strength there steals
    O'er valley and o'er hill
The glad shout of a nation, when it feels
Its monarch worthy of his crown. Then seals
Each one his lips, while he his wish reveals :
    " It is my Sovereign Will,

Who proves himself the doughtiest in the land
Hath for reward my daughter Edith's hand ;
        Ope ye the lists ! "


Forth from the crowd rode out a knight
        Upon a coal-black steed ;
His armour, bruised in many a fight,
Was of wrought iron, black as night,
And from his helmet, waving bright,
        A scarlet plume was freed ;
All else from helm to iron spur
Was black as wing of scavenger.


His sturdy war-steed, stoutly made,
        His burden seemed to spurn,
And well his rider's seat displayed
        By many a prance and turn ;
And on his ponderous iron shield
(Weapon which he alone could wield)
In tall red letters stood revealed,
        That all who saw might learn,
Those flaming letters side by side,
Spell out his haughty motto, " Pride."


Then, rising in his stirrups high,
        He shakes his quiv'ring lance ;
Harsh rings his hoarse and boastful cry,
        And wild his courser's prance :—
' My name is Pride.  I dare you all,
By this good lance, beneath this castle wall,
Before my king, his peers, and courtiers all,
        And yonder maid's sweet glance ;
For never yet in battle, list, or fight,
Have I my equal found in any knight !

The fight was fierce ; the fight was hard and long ;
　　But now the fray is o'er ;
And many a warrior, skilled, and brave, and strong,
　　Lies on that sanded floor ;
And leaning hard upon his battleaxe
To gain the strength his wounded body lacks,
Stands Pride alone, amidst those bloody tracks
　　All dyed with blood and gore.
His boast not vain ; for in that awful fight
Not one was found to prove the better knight.

His armour broke, his helm clove to the eyes,
　　The gay plume cut away,
His gallant steed lifeless beside him lies,
　　Where many another lay ;
And in those blood-stained lists, 'midst shattered spears
And groans of dying men and women's tears,
His haughty head once more he proudly rears
　　The Victor of to-day !
By sheer indomitable will he conquers pain
And mounts another steed to fight again.

The first three knights who fell before his sword—
　　The awful blade of Pride—
Greed, Meanness, Avarice, each a mighty lord,
　　Now silent side by side.
Honour and Truth, both fighting nobly, fell ;
Passion, a very demon, hot from Hell.
Friendship, a stout old knight, who bore him well
　　And clove the helm of Pride ;
Falsehood, a cunning knave, wily, and skilled at feint.
Old Generosity, Young Self-Restraint.

All these he slew, and many minor foes
　　Who strove to stem his wrath.
And now his iron gauntlet down he throws,
　　But not a knight comes forth :

Then with a mighty shout the people cry,
" There now remains no knight who dares to try
His maiden shield against, in chivalry,
    The warrior of the North.
Redeem, O King, thy pledge, and let us see
The victor wed the maid of high degree ! "

Then up the monarch rose, and strove to speak
    Amidst that deafening roar,
And pale as death again grew Edith's cheek,
    And wilder than before
Her eyes sought vainly in that heaving crowd
For him to whom her secret troth was vowed,
And, seeing nought, her golden head she bowed
    To Fate's relentless law ;
When from yon distant hills, and grove of trees,
A silver note comes floating on the breeze.

So loud, so clear, so silvery it broke
    Upon the ears of all,
That in the mind of Pride a fear it woke
    That perhaps his star might fall ;
Then, bursting thro' the trees at headlong speed,
A warrior mounted on a snow-white steed
Is seen : and Edith's heart is freed
    From thoughts which did appal,
And, as the evening sun falls on his golden mail,
No eyes can look thereon and yet not quail.

The lists are reached, he reins his panting steed
    Beneath the monarch's stand,            .
And with a glance which well his cause doth plead,
    Surveys the lovely band ;
Then from his courser swiftly doth alight,
And there before her eyes, and in their sight,
Lifting the gauntlet of the man of might,
    Restores it to his hand.

Then with an oath Pride roars in wrathful need :—
"Bring me fresh armour and another steed."

Now Pride is mounted, and the trumpets sound ;
    The lances are in rest ;
The stallions gallop forward with a bound ;
    Bent is each knightly crest.
They meet—the shock—the deadlock—and the people's
    shout ;
But neither falls from his high saddle out
Tho' two good lances strew the ground about.
    Can neither prove him best ?
Without there !  Bring fresh lances to each knight
Sound trump again, and onward with the fight.

Again they meet.  Again each lance is split,
    Again fresh steel is brought.
What ho !  Fresh topic for the minstrel's wit
    How gallantly they fought !
Once more another lance, once more the shock,
The crash of steel on steel : I see one rock,
Rock in his saddle, and fall headlong down,
    'Tis Pride.  His fall is wrought ;
He falls upon the sand—that mighty lord—
Then leaps upon his feet, and draws his sword.

Now, noble minstrel, string thy tuneful lyre
    And sing thy battle lay.
The stranger knight springs off his steed of fire,
    And flings his lance away ;
Then, man to man, they stand upon the sand ;
Never in all the annals of the land
Such fight was fought, and well each strong right hand
    Makes his good broadsword play.
But not a sound is heard save steel on steel .
Or the sharp gasp when back both champions reel.

But quickly they recover, and again
    Fiercer the battle grows,
And blows are showered thick as April rain,
    Yet neither backward goes.
But, see ! Oh, Fate ! Pride one false pass has made
And swift as thought the stranger's glittering blade
Circles around the head defenceless laid
    And batters down his foe's,
Crashes thro' helm and visor to the brain,
And fairly cleaves the head of Pride in twain.

'Tis done. The ruddy life-blood stains the ground,
    And Pride at length is dead.
Then once again the murmur flies around ;
    " Who is this knight ? " they said.
" Who is this stranger clad in golden mail,
Before whose steel our doughtiest champions quail,
Who rides yon Arab with the flowing tail ?
    Let him unbar his head."
But when he heard them, and unbarred his head,
" 'Tis but a boy ! " in wonderment they said.

A boy, but an Apollo of a boy !
    He stood before the King,
His handsome face diffused with love and joy,
    And in his hand a ring ;
His hazel eyes sparkling with keen delight,
His armour bruised and dinted in the fight,
He looked the very picture of a knight ;
    He said, " This ring I bring,
Oh, king ! I now make my demand :
Bestow on me thy peerless Edith's hand !

" My name is Love, they call me the Sublime,
    My wings are Mirth and Joy ;
It is my fate all thro' existing time
    Always to be a boy.

'Tis not my maiden field, for I have fought
Since Time, and Earth, and all things first were brought
From Chaos ; and this sword has bought
    Full many a victory.
I have a few more fights ; then shall be given to me
All things, and I shall rule eternally."

So, near the lists, where so much blood was shed,
Love and the maid of high degree were wed.

But Love arose from by his loved one's side
    And spoke unto the King,
And said, " I have a balm that, whatsoe'er betide,
    Will back the life-blood bring."
Then quoth the monarch, eagerly :—
" Restore my fallen knights to me ! "

Then Love stepped down, and with his healing balm
    Gently closed up the wounds in Friendship's side ;
Then with his silver trumpet broke the calm,
    And Friendship rose from by the corpse of Pride ;

And Generosity and Self-Restraint he cured,
And Truth and Honour who death had endured ;
But Meanness, Falsehood, Passion, Pride, and Greed,
Were left with Avarice, hungry crows to feed,
Till some one, finding all these slaves of sin,
Dug a big hole, and flung such carrion in.

# A JINGLE FOR MUSIC.

" That is best which liest nearest
Shape from that thy work of Art."

SAID the Master : "Build the Palace
 From the stones which lie around,
From the blocks which are the nearest
 Lying strewn upon the ground ;
Time will test which is best—
Blocks which we have never tested
 Or the stones which lie around."

So they worked and built the Palace
 From the stones which lay around,
From the blocks which were the nearest
 Lying strewn upon the ground ;
'Till the last block was cast
And a stately palace builded
 From the stones which lay around.

Let us build a stately nation
 From the love that lies around,
From the love, and truth, and honour
 Which is nearest to be found !
Till the shout echoes out :
" Lo ! the strength that made the Nation
 Was the Love that girt her round."

# THE RUSSIAN ADVANCE.

THE roll of drums, the bugle peal,
  The clink of spurs, and a martial tread,
The prance of steeds, the rumbling wheel
  Of cannon.  The sheen their bayonets shed
Glittering keen in the morning red ;
  While the Russian Eagles float o'erhead.

Lurid the danger signals glow,
  And thicker gather the clouds of war,
And rumours which tell of the coming foe—
  Ill-omened harbingers—fly before ;
And then with a dim and distant roar,      ,
  Which the echoing hills again repeat,
Like the boom of the surf on some rock-bound shore,
  The thunder of thousands of marching feet.

Onward they come in the morning gray,
  Southwards the tides of their legions roll—
In the gloomiest hour of Britannia's day,
  Sullenly South to their Indian goal—
Proudly and loudly their drummers play ;
  Proudly and loudly their bugles peal ;
But stern and stubborn to bar the way
  Stands a bristling wall of British steel.

## TO THE AUTHOR OF "MORNA LEE."

A GREAT thought clothed with living words
    That burn upon the heart and brain,
A note struck on Love's strongest chords—
    Nor struck in vain.

Not loud, but deep : 'mystic song
    Far-echoing thro' the Halls of Thought,
With weird vibrations that belong
    To the Unsought.

Trembling upon the verge of things
    Seen dimly, or in broken gleams,
Like Unknown Truths whose radiant wings
    Brighten our dreams.

A voice which from the air above
    Speaks to all hearts ; a fervid breath
Of faith unshaken ; and a love
    Stronger than Death.

# THE SPIRIT OF NATURE.

O Genius of the Universe !
In every soft or freshening breeze
Which stirs the branches of the trees,
I hear the music of thy voice—
The rhythm of a mystic song
Whose cadence haunts the spirit long,
And bids the shades of care disperse,
And makes the restless heart rejoice ;
For, lo ! the presence of a power
Unseen, but felt, hangs o'er the hour ;
Soft as the breeze which evening brings
I hear the rustle of its wings ;
And feel the shadow of its might
Like the calm silence of the night.

O Spirit of the Wilderness,
Solemn and grand and passionless !
Thy voice is in the winds that roam
Without a resting-place or home ;
Thy garb is Nature's loveliness.
In the stern tempest's sullen roar
I hear thy songs of triumph soar ;
In the soft breeze that sinks and dies
The swell of tender harmonies ;
And wild and musical and free
I feel their subtle influence steal
And cast a glamour over me,
Until I cry with fierce appeal :
" Would that my restless heart could be
Light as the breezes, and as free ! "

# THE LAND OF SHADOWS.

"That undiscovered country from whose bourn
No traveller returns."

THERE is a land from whose mysterious shore
No echoes can return to us again ;
No sign, no sound, of gladness or of pain
Tell of the myriads who have gone before.

There is a stream beneath whose turbid wave
Millions have sunk, and millions yet shall sink ;
Dark are the gath'ring shades upon the brink
Unknown the shore its utmost waters lave.

But in the death-like silence of the night,
When the long shadows deepen near and far,
'Tis strange to meditate how frail a bar
Severs the Finite from the Infinite.

Beside the darksome margin of that stream
We, each, shall stand unaided and alone
Upon the trembling verge of things unknown,
Where all the Past shall melt as doth a dream.

A dream ! Why not ? Have we not dreamt before ?
Flashes of recognition glimmer through—
The new dreams are the old, the old the new,
And we, in visions, pass from shore to shore.

Vague influences waken, and a ray
Illumes the hidden chambers of the mind—
Echoes and forms and faces left behind
In some existence that has passed away,

Faint dreams, dim memories of bygone things
 Not wholly unfamiliar, for they seem
 The reflex of some long-forgotten dream
Whose light and sweetness still around us clings.

Such lights will flash and vanish : as we glance
 We scarce can read the truths their beams illume ;
 We are but children groping through the gloom,
And all our knowledge is but ignorance.

But from the Future, from that silent sphere,
 That Shadowland no mortal foot shall tread,
 Cometh no sign, no whisper, of the dead ;
No sound, no voice, no echo to the ear ;

No answer save the silence.  And the veil
 Is lifted not, nor shall be, till we stand
 Within the confines of that Shadowland
Upon whose verge the stoutest spirits quail.

Oh, well for him who hears with steadfast soul,
 When, like the muffled beating of a drum,
 The voice of those dark waters whispers " Come,"
Nor fears the brink where the deep shadows roll.

Dogmas and creeds will vanish ; but the Power
 Which permeates Nature, whose diviner plan
 Is shadowed dimly in the heart of man,
Will still uphold his soul in that stern hour.

That Power whose work is endless—never done—
 That breathes in all things in those realms unknown,
 Will bind the world's religions in one zone,
And blend the creeds of all men into one.

# LOVE.

Love knows no law save love alone. It springs
From the eternal majesty of God,
From the infinity of God Himself,
Essence of Life, the Sov'reignty supreme
Which bends our natures to a higher Will ;
And, in the fadeless bowers of Paradise
Where amaranth flowers and thornless roses bloom,
Where angels tread the starry floors of Heaven,
In the celestial harmonies that roll
Vibrating thro' the vast ethereal spheres,
Unfathomable spaces of futurity,
Love's voice goes forth unchallenged, absolute,
Reigning thro' all—for God Himself is Love.
O Power Illimitable ! Power Divine !
That, deathless, burst th' enthralling bonds of Death,
And, rising, soared beyond th' eternal stars,
On thy strong pinions bear our spirits up,
So may we wear thro' all this maze of Life,
Thro' the dark shadows of terrestrial days,
The jewel of imperishable love
That Time and Death and Sorrow cannot dim.

## ANIMUS NON MORTALIS EST.

WHERE are they now—the poets of all time,
Who charmed·the world with melody and rhyme,
  And thoughts sublime and deep ?
Think'st thou they have expired ?  No.  He who said
Their torch is quenched, and they are cold and dead,
  Hath lied—they do but sleep.

And in another purer atmosphere,
Their songs shall peal more sweetly and more clear
  Than e'en they did on earth ;
And gath'ring strength from what we cannot see
Shall swell in one great burst of harmony,
  With wider nobler girth.

# WAR.

IMPERIOUS Goddess ! proud Bellona ! stay,
So I may strive to read thy secret heart ;
Tear from thy cruel face the mask away,
And let men see thee as thou really art.
That lofty air, that brave yet scornful smile,
But hides the pitiless stern features 'neath
The mask by which thou dost men's hearts beguile
To risk their lives to win thy laurel-wreath.
Thy gorgeous pageantry, thy nodding plumes,
The martial music's glorious stirring swell,
Are but the shrouds for twice ten thousand tombs—
For twice ten thousand but Death's solemn knell.
Two hostile hosts ablaze with glittering steel ;
The thunder of artillery ; the shock
Of charging squadrons ; the proud bugle-peal—
Clear, loud, yet silvery, as tho' to mock
Some dying soldier's agonized appeal
To Heaven for mercy ; then the tiny square,
Lost in the dense gray haze of battle-cloud
While charging hordes press round it everywhere,
Still sternly stubborn—but as sternly proud,
Defiant, and immovable—and like the rock
O'er which old Ocean's mountain billows tear,
Break, burst in thunder, yet can not
Move from its native fastnesses one jot.
And men—with quickened senses as they hear
The bugle-call, the clash as steel meets steel,

And see their native banner's crest uprear
High o'er them—then can only feel,
As the battalions of the foe appear
In columned grandeur nearer and more near,
Their pulses throb, and the warm life-blood glow,
And care for nought save victory o'er the foe.
Thus ever, Goddess ! when with naked sword
Thou standest, crying " Glory—onward go ! "
Men have been ready to obey thy word,
Nor count the odds, nor heed that blood must flow ;
And so it is, has been, will be, thy plan
So long as earth is earth, and man is man.


That is one side the picture ; but I would—
If so be that I can a landscape draw—
Depict both light and shade, as artist should,
And paint the awful shades of glorious war.
I see the moonlight on the battle-field
When all is silent and the fight is o'er,
And there Death's harvest ; 'tis a mighty yield,
Yet hath he reaped such yields full oft before.
And there they lie—not singly, but in heaps,
In ghastly heaps ; the dying with the dead
All intermingled—while the cold wind sweeps
Across and moans their requiem overhead.
And this is War ! Great, glorious, awful War !—
Whose praises poets still are wont to sing—
With all its pomp, and majesty, and awe !
Yet, to my mind, it seems a gruesome thing
To think that for each wretch maimed, wounded, torn
By shot, and left stark dead upon the plain,
Some loving hearts (tho' far away) must mourn—
Must weep in bitterness—must weep in vain.
" He dies with honour who doth fall in war,"
They say, and count the heroes of the strife.

Can this, the loved one to his home restore,
Or fill his nostrils with the breath of life ?
A warrior's grave they deck with laurel leaf,
And honour him whose honour knew no stain,
But to his nearest (in their hopeless grief),
The laurel fades—the cypress will remain.
Imperious Goddess ! when it is thy plan
With martial majesty to set the task
For man to battle with his brother man,
Show each thy countenance—without the mask.

# TO THE NEW YEAR.

Go forth, O Year, bearing our destinies—
The hopes, joys, sorrows, and the happiness
Which make the sum of our existence here !
The burden of all human life and death
Is on thy shoulders, and from day to day
Will broaden as thy steps draw nearer home.
Lift then thy torch of promise and fair hope
To light the millions on their onward march ;
And, if thy reign be wise, remember this,—
No lesser power than Love can rule a world
Of such complexity of end and aim.

# THE SORREL MARE.

I SAW an angler by a stream
  Which flowed on gently, rippling by,
And at every sound a watchful gleam
  Came and went in his hazel eye ;
And every day for a week or two
In that self-same spot his line he threw.

  .    .    .    .    .    .

There is an old manor-house not far away,
  With many a quaint old gateway and tower,
And every morn at the break of day,
  Ere the sun has risen in all his power,
A gray old groom on a sorrel mare
Comes riding through the gateway there.

  .    .    .    .    .    .

In the town hard by, at the " Boar's Head " sign
  (A tavern where liquor is cheap and good),
Some Roundhead soldiers over their wine
  Are yarning as only old comrades could ;
And at last some one—old Praise-the-Lord Brown—
Begins running his comrades' horses down.

" There is no horse like my stallion gray
  From Yorkshire's moors to old London town
For speed and strength, and courage and stay ;
  No racer in England can gallop him down !
Ho ! comrades all, in a flagon of ale
Here's health and long life to old Martingale ! "

Then up they stand and their glasses clink ;
" Here's health to old Martingale ! " they say ;
And down goes the liquor without a shrink
As with jovial faces the toast they drink
Of Praise-the-Lord Brown's old stallion gray.
" Ho, fools ! " think I ; " none of you, I swear,
Have seen the stride of that sorrel mare ! "

.       .      .      .      .      .

A day or so after, the news flies round—
" The Roundheads have captured Charles the King ! "
The Crop-ears, who've got him safe and sound,
Will past the Manor their prisoner bring.
But still as before (what I'm telling is true)
In that self-same spot that angler threw.

They come ! they come ! those crop-eared curs ;
And he in the middle must be the King ;
I hear horses tramp, and the jingle of spurs,
As 'neath their riders the chargers spring ;
But that angler bold is quite unconcerned,
Nor have I as yet his secret learned.

But see ! They pass quite close to the brook,
And the angler turns to see them go by ;
He makes a swift sign with a meaning look,
And I see the King has caught his eye ;
But of all that crowd none the sign did see
Save I and the King and that angler free.

They pass, and the angler unscrews his rod ;
His fishing is done for a good long while ;
He picks up his basket from off the sod,
And goes away with a curious smile.
But what is that close to the hedge over there ?
Zounds ! It's old Giles on the sorrel mare !

By good St. George ! 'twas a sight to see
  When the fisher let go his rod and line
And the mare from old Tom got nearly free,
  As she whinnied and pranced and commenced to
    whine.
Ah ! well, my bonny, you knew who was there ;
And you've carried that fisher before, I swear !

     .     .     .     .

They talk for a minute—he and old Giles—
  While the mare puts her muzzle right into his hand ;
" Is she fit," he asks, with one of his smiles,
  " To carry me down to Dover's sands ? "
" Fit ?  Yes," says Tom ; "and further than that,
If she ain't, Sir Fulke, I'll eat my hat."


One foot's in the stirrup—but " Hist ! can't ye hear ? "
  And back 'midst the oak trees the cavalier strode.
" I hear a clatter of hoofs so near,
  They must be coming right down the road ;
By our Lady ! a troop !—and Praise-the-Lord Brown !
Zounds !  He's found me out, and will run me down ! "


Now into the saddle without a word,
  And turn her head for Dover's sand ;
And over the fence she flies like a bird,
  And down the road comes that crop-eared band ;
But riding first, on his stallion gray,
Old Praise-the-Lord Brown shows his men the way.


" There he goes ! " yells Brown : " the spy ! the spy !
  The plagues of Egypt be on his head ;
And fifty pounds of my pay give I
  To the man who catches him 'live or dead ! "
" Aha ! " chuckles Giles from behind the hedge,
" Your turtle's too close to the water's edge ! "

Then over the hedge with a bound they go ;
  The gray horse high o'er the blackthorn sped ;
They are racing now and their hands are low,
  But the chase is already two fields ahead.
Quoth Giles to himself, " A brave mount, I declare,
But 'twill take a better to catch the mare ! "


Sir Fulke stands up in his stirrups high,
  And glances round and waves his hand ;
He has gained every stride—three fields now lie
  'Twixt the sorrel mare and that crop-eared band ;
But leading his comrades by half a field
Steadily onwards the gray horse stealed.


O ! 'tis gallant to ride on a mare like Bess !
  Firm turf beneath, and a gaining stride ;
And never she seemed to feel work less
  As he patted her neck with honest pride ;
Like clockwork she galloped, like lightning flew
Thro' the lush grass heavy with diamond dew.


But straight ahead looms a bullfinch fence,
  Black and gaunt with a stiff oak rail ;
He steadies the mare ; she knows his sense—
  She shortens her stride yet does not quail ;
O'er the rasping spires like a dart she sped :
He needs such cattle who rides for his head !


" O my Bessie ! " he cries, exulting now,
  As he slackens speed ; he must save her strength :
He wipes the sweat from his wringing brow
  And takes up a hole in his stirrup's length ;
Full well he knew had she failed him there
It had been his last ride on his sorrel mare.

But the gray is a gallant horse and true—
   Over timber or grass he is hard to beat—
And the rider who steers him is dauntless too,
   With an iron nerve and a faultless seat :
Scarce stirred the tips of the bullfinch tall
As he rose like a bird o'er that thorny wall.


Sir Fulke has dallied a little too long
   And the stallion behind him can travel and stay ;
But he laughs, for the sorrel is galloping strong,
   And he shouts to Brown in his careless way :—
" The mare 'gainst the gray for a flagon of sack,
And my head is the stake if you take me back ! "


And now o'er timber, and now o'er grass,
   O'er plough, and stubble, and field, and fen,
O'er blackthorn walls like a flash they pass,
   Eager horses and reckless men ;
As she tops the ditch by the slope of the hill,
Three fields ahead she is leading still.


With arching neck and a length'ning stride
   Splashed and spattered with foam and mire,
She does not flinch where the brook is wide ;
   Where the clay is softest she does not tire ;
The heart that ne'er quailed in the martial strife
Will not fail him now when he rides for his life.


The old mill race runs swift and deep,
   He can hear the swollen waters roar ;
He can see the current eddy and sweep,
   But safety lies on the farther shore :
Bold is the rider and staunch the mare
Who faces the breadth of its waters there.

But Sir Fulke is calm, if the stream is wide ;
  His hand is steady, his face is set ;
The heart that danger has proved and tried
  In chase and battle is dauntless yet :
He laughs as he thinks of the troopers near,
She is sound as a bell, she can jump like a deer.


From bank to bank thirty feet if an inch !
  —The thud of her hoofs is a steadier beat ;—
She pricks her ears, but she does not flinch ;
  He settles down with a firmer seat :
A swift rush—a wild bound—she shoots thro' the air
And lands him safe with a foot to spare.


" Safe !   Safe at last !   Long live King Charles !
  I will toast him in Dover ere set of sun ;
Baffled by Bess be all crop-eared carles,
  Who follow her heels in a hunting run ;
An old jack-boot and a flagon of ale
Is all I would offer for Martingale."


" Not so ! " quoth old Brown, " I've another Bess here,
  We'll prove which is best, as you're anxious to try."
The carbine was true, and the target was near,
  And keen down the barrel he laid his eye :
A flash—a report—and an agonized scream—
And the sorrel lay, dying, across the stream.


" Dying ?   Not *dying*, but *dead !*   Bess is gone,
  And never again will that gallant heart beat !
Oh, never again on her back to be borne !
  Oh, never again her soft whinnies to greet !
Be it rider or horse, be it soul or clay,
No braver spirit has passed away.

" There she lies with her glossy coat muddy and red,
    And those rich brown eyes glazed which so brightly
    could shine ;
A vile Crop-ear's bullet has shattered her head
Who gave up her young life a forfeit for mine !
Oh, Praise-the-Lord Brown, you've a long score to pay ;
And I'll pay it with interest settling day ! "

No need now, ye bullies, for further pursuit :
    They forded the stream and arrested their prey.
No answer he gives them ; his strong voice is mute ;
    And their summons to rise up he does not obey :
But sits still like one stunned, with her head on his knees,
And the dead sorrel mare is the sole thing he sees.

Then slowly he rises and o'er her does stand,
    His handsome face wearing a dull look of pain,
As he stoops o'er her corse, with his knife in his hand,
    And severs a lock from her beautiful mane ;
Then they bind him and carry him off to the town,
But he speaks not a word, and looks moodily down.
            .    .    .    .    .    .

Sir Fulke was not murdered, nor hanged as a spy ;
    Though he stood before Cromwell and spoke for his king ;
But was doomed for long years in a prison to lie,
    Till from over the water the glad news took wing ;
And Praise-the-Lord Brown, in a drunken fray,
Was shot through the head on his stallion gray.
            .    .    .    .    .    .

To the Second King Charles now the English look ;
    To Sir Fulke the manor has been restored ;
His boys now fish in the rippling brook,
    Or play at men with their father's sword ;
And oft by old Giles is the story told
Of the sorrel mare Bess and her rider bold.

THE END.

The Gresham Press,

UNWIN BROTHERS

CHILWORTH AND LONDON.

*A Catalogue of American and Foreign Books Published or Imported by* MESSRS. SAMPSON LOW & CO. *can be had on application.*

*St. Dunstan's House, Fetter Lane, Fleet Street, London,*
*October,* 1889.

# 𝔄 𝔖𝔢𝔩𝔢𝔠𝔱𝔦𝔬𝔫 𝔣𝔯𝔬𝔪 𝔱𝔥𝔢 𝔏𝔦𝔰𝔱 𝔬𝔣 𝔅𝔬𝔬𝔨𝔰

PUBLISHED BY

## SAMPSON LOW, MARSTON, SEARLE, & RIVINGTON,

*LIMITED.*

**Low's Standard Novels,** page 17.
**Low's Standard Books for Boys,** page 18.
**Low's Standard Series,** page 19.
**Sea Stories,** by W. CLARK RUSSELL, page 26.

### ALPHABETICAL LIST.

*ABBEY and Parsons, Quiet life.* From drawings ; the motive by Austin Dobson, 4to.

*Abney (W. de W.) and Cunningham. Pioneers of the Alps.* With photogravure portraits of guides. Imp. 8vo, gilt top, 21s.

*Adam (G. Mercer) and Wetherald. An Algonquin Maiden.* Crown 8vo, 5s.

*Alcott. Works of the late Miss Louisa May Alcott :—*
Aunt Jo's Scrap-bag. Cloth, 2s.
Eight Cousins. Illustrated, 2s.; cloth gilt, 3s. 6d.
Jack and Jill. Illustrated, 2s.; cloth gilt, 3s. 6d.
Jo's Boys. 5s.
Jimmy's Cruise in the Pinafore, &c. Illustrated, cloth, 2s.; gilt edges, 3s. 6d.
Little Men. Double vol., 2s.; cloth, gilt edges, 3s. 6d.
Little Women. 1s. } 1 vol., cloth, 2s. ; larger ed., gilt
Little Women Wedded. 1s. }     edges, 3s. 6d.
Old-fashioned Girl. 2s.; cloth, gilt edges, 3s. 6d.
Rose in Bloom. 2s.; cloth gilt, 3s. 6d.
Shawl Straps. Cloth, 2s.
Silver Pitchers. Cloth, gilt edges, 3s. 6d.
Under the Lilacs. Illustrated, 2s.; cloth gilt, 5s.
Work : a Story of Experience. 1s. } 1 vol., cloth, gilt
—— Its Sequel, " Beginning Again." 1s. }   edges, 3s. 6d.
—— *Life, Letters and Journals.* By EDNAH D. CHENEY. Cr. 8vo, 6s.
—— See also "Low's Standard Series."

*Alden (W. L.) Adventures of Jimmy Brown, written by himself.* Illustrated. Small crown 8vo, cloth, 2s.

—— *Trying to find Europe.* Illus., crown 8vo, 5s.

A

*Aiger* (*J. G.*) *Englishmen in the French Revolution*, cr. 8vo, 7s. 6d.
*Amateur Angler's Days in Dove Dale : Three Weeks' Holiday* in 1884. By E. M. 1s. 6d. ; boards, 1s. ; large paper, 5s.
*Andersen. Fairy Tales.* An entirely new Translation. With over 500 Illustrations by Scandinavian Artists. Small 4to, 6s.
*Anderson* (*W.*) *Pictorial Arts of Japan.* With 80 full-page and other Plates, 16 of them in Colours. Large imp. 4to, £8 8s. (in four folio parts, £2 2s. each) ; Artists' Proofs, £12 12s.
*Angling.* See Amateur, "Cutcliffe," "Fennell," "Halford," "Hamilton," "Martin," "Orvis," "Pennell," "Pritt," "Senior," "Stevens," "Theakston," "Walton," "Wells," and "Willis-Bund."
*Arnold* (*R.*) *Ammonia and Ammonium Compounds.* Translated, illus., crown 8vo, 5s.
*Art Education.* See "Biographies," "D'Anvers," "Illustrated Text Books," "Mollett's Dictionary."
*Artistic Japan.* Illustrated with Coloured Plates. Monthly. Royal 4to, 2s.; vol. I., 15s.; II., roy. 4to., 15s.
*Ashe* (*R. P.*) *Two Kings of Uganda ; Six Years in E. Equatorial Africa.* Crown 8vo, 6s.
*Attwell* (*Prof.*) *The Italian Masters.* Crown 8vo, 3s. 6d.
*Audsley* (*G. A.*) *Handbook of the Organ.* Imperial 8vo, top edge gilt, 31s. 6d.; large paper, 63s.
————— *Ornamental Arts of Japan.* 90 Plates, 74 in Colours and Gold, with General and Descriptive Text. 2 vols., folio, £15 15s.; in specally designed leather, £23 2s.
————— *The Art of Chromo-Lithography.* Coloured Plates and Text. Folio, 63s.

*B*ACON (*Delia*) *Biography, with Letters of Carlyle, Emerson*, &c. Crown 8vo, 10s. 6d.
*Baddeley* (*W. St. Clair*) *Tchay and Chianti.* Small 8vo, 5s.
————— *Travel-tide.* Small post 8vo, 7s. 6d.
*Baldwin* (*James*) *Story of Siegfried.* 6s.
————— *Story of the Golden Age.* Illustrated by HOWARD PYLE. Crown 8vo, 6s.
————— *Story of Roland.* Crown 8vo, 6s.
*Bamford* (*A. J.*) *Turbans and Tails.* Sketches in the Unromantic East. Crown 8vo, 7s. 6d.
*Barlow* (*Alfred*) *Weaving by Hand and by Power.* With several hundred Illustrations. Third Edition, royal 8vo, £1 5s.
*Barlow* (*P. W.*) *Kaipara, Experiences of a Settler in N. New* Zealand. Illust., crown 8vo, 6s.
*Bassett* (*F. S.*) *Legends and Superstitions of the Sea.* 7s. 6d.

# THE BAYARD SERIES.

Edited by the late J. HAIN FRISWELL.

Comprising Pleasure Books of Literature produced in the Choicest Style.

"We can hardly imagine better books for boys to read or for men to ponder over."—*Times.*

*Price 2s. 6d. each Volume, complete in itself, flexible cloth extra, gilt edges, with silk Headbands and Registers.*

The Story of the Chevalier Bayard.
Joinville's St. Louis of France.
The Essays of Abraham Cowley.
Abdallah. By Edouard Laboullaye.
Napoleon, Table-Talk and Opinions.
Words of Wellington.
Johnson's Rasselas. With Notes.
Hazlitt's Round Table.
The Religio Medici, Hydriotaphia, &c. By Sir Thomas Browne, Knt.
Coleridge's Christabel, &c. With Preface by Algernon C. Swinburne.
Ballad Poetry of the Affections. By Robert Buchanan.

Lord Chesterfield's Letters, Sentences, and Maxims. With Essay by Sainte-Beuve.
The King and the Commons. Cavalier and Puritan Songs.
Vathek. By William Beckford.
Essays in Mosaic. By Ballantyne.
My Uncle Toby ; his Story and his Friends. By P. Fitzgerald.
Reflections of Rochefoucauld.
Socrates : Memoirs for English Readers from Xenophon's Memorabilia. By Edw. Levien.
Prince Albert's Golden Precepts.

*A Case containing 12 Volumes, price 31s. 6d.; or the Case separately, price 3s. 6d.*

*Beaugrand (C.) Walks Abroad of Two Young Naturalists.* By D. SHARP. Illust., 8vo, 7s. 6d.

*Beecher (H. W.) Authentic Biography, and Diary.* Ill. 8vo, 21s.

*Behnke and Browne. Child's Voice: its Treatment with regard* to After Development. Small 8vo, 3s. 6d.

*Bell (H. H. J.) Obeah : Negro Superstition in the West Indies.* Crown 8vo, 2s. 6d.

*Beyschlag. Female Costume Figures of various Centuries.* 12 reproductions of pastel designs in portfolio, imperial. 21s.

*Bickerdyke (J.) Irish Midsummer Night's Dream.* Illus. by E. M. Cox. Crown 8vo, 1s. 6d. ; boards, 1s.

*Bickersteth (Bishop E. H.) Clergyman in his Home.* 1s.

—————— *Evangelical Churchmanship.* 1s.

—————— *From Year to Year: Original Poetical Pieces.* Small post 8vo, 3s. 6d. ; roan, 6s. and 5s.; calf or morocco, 10s. 6d.

—————— *The Master's Home-Call.* N. ed. 32mo, cloth gilt, 1s.

—————— *The Master's Will.* A Funeral Sermon preached on the Death of Mrs. S. Gurney Buxton. Sewn, 6d. ; cloth gilt, 1s.

—————— *The Reef, and other Parables.* Crown 8vo, 2s. 6d.

—————— *Shadow of the Rock.* Select Religious Poetry. 2s. 6d.

—————— *Shadowed Home and the Light Beyond.* 5s.

—————— See also " Hymnal Companion."

A 2

*Biographies of the Great Artists* (*Illustrated*). Crown 8vo, emblematical binding, 3*s*. 6*d*. per volume, except where the price is given.

Claude le Lorrain, by Owen J. Dullea.
Correggio, by M. E. Heaton. 2*s*. 6*d*.
Della Robbia and Cellini. 2*s*. 6*d*.
Albrecht Dürer, by R. F. Heath.
Figure Painters of Holland.
Fra Angelico, Masaccio, and Botticelli.
Fra Bartolommeo, Albertinelli, and Andrea del Sarto.
Gainsborough and Constable.
Ghiberti and Donatello. 2*s*. 6*d*.
Giotto, by Harry Quilter.
Hans Holbein, by Joseph Cundall.
Hogarth, by Austin Dobson.
Landseer, by F. G. Stevens.
Lawrence and Romney, by Lord Ronald Gower. 2*s*. 6*d*.
Leonardo da Vinci.
Little Masters of Germany, by W. B. Scott.

Mantegna and Francia.
Meissonier, by J. W. Mollett. 2*s*. 6*d*.
Michelangelo Buonarotti, by Clément.
Murillo, by Ellen E. Minor. 2*s*. 6*d*.
Overbeck, by J. B. Atkinson.
Raphael, by N. D'Anvers.
Rembrandt, by J. W. Mollett.
Reynolds, by F. S. Pulling.
Rubens, by C. W. Kett.
Tintoretto, by W. R. Osler.
Titian, by R. F. Heath.
Turner, by Cosmo Monkhouse.
Vandyck and Hals, by P. R. Head.
Velasquez, by E. Stowe.
Vernet and Delaroche, by J. Rees.
Watteau, by J. W. Mollett. 2*s*. 6*d*.
Wilkie, by J. W. Mollett.

IN PREPARATION.

Barbizon School, by J. W. Mollett.
Cox and De Wint, Lives and Works.
George Cruikshank, Life and Works.

Miniature Painters of Eng. School.
Mulready Memorials, by Stephens.
Van de Velde and the Dutch Painters.

*Bird* (*F. J.*) *American Practical Dyer's Companion.* 8vo, 42*s*.

────── (*H. E.*) *Chess Practice.* 8vo, 2*s*. 6*d*.

*Black* (*Robert*) *Horse Racing in France : a History.* 8vo, 14*s*.

────── See also CICERO.

*Black* (*W.*) *Penance of John Logan, and other Tales.* Crown 8vo, 10*s*. 6*d*.

──────See also " Low's Standard Library."

*Blackburn* (*Charles F.*) *Hints on Catalogue Titles and Index* Entries, with a Vocabulary of Terms and Abbreviations, chiefly from Foreign Catalogues. Royal 8vo, 14*s*.

*Blackburn* (*Henry*) *Art in the Mountains, the Oberammergau* Passion Play. New ed., corrected to date, 8vo, 5*s*.

────── *Breton Folk.* With 171 Illust. by RANDOLPH CALDECOTT Imperial 8vo, gilt edges, 21*s*. ; plainer binding, 10*s*. 6*d*.

────── *Pyrenees.* Illustrated by GUSTAVE DORÉ, corrected to 1881. Crown 8vo, 7*s*. 6*d*. See also CALDECOTT.

*Blackmore* (*R. D.*) *Kit and Kitty.* A novel. 3 vols., crown 8vo, 31*s*. 6*d*.

────── *Lorna Doone. Édition de luxe.* Crown 4to, very numerous Illustrations, cloth, gilt edges, 31*s*. 6*d*.; parchment, uncut, top gilt, 35*s*. ; new issue, plainer, 21*s*.

────── *Novels.* See also " Low's Standard Novels."

*Blackmore (R. D.) Springhaven.* Illust. by PARSONS and BARNARD. Sq. 8vo, 12*s.*; new edition, 7*s.* 6*d.*

*Blaikie (William) How to get Strong and how to Stay so.* Rational, Physical, Gymnastic, &c., Exercises. Illust., sm. post 8vo, 5*s.*

———— *Sound Bodies for our Boys and Girls.* 16mo, 2*s.* 6*d.*

*Bonwick. British Colonies.* Asia, 1*s.*; Africa, 1*s.*; America, 1*s.*; Australasia, 1*s.* One vol., cloth, 5*s.*

*Bosanquet (Rev. C.) Blossoms from the King's Garden : Sermons* for Children. 2nd Edition, small post 8vo, cloth extra, 6*s.*

———— *Jehoshaphat ; or, Sunlight and Clouds.* 1*s.*

*Bowden (H.; Miss) Witch of the Atlas : a ballooning story,* Crown 8vo, 6*s.*

*Bower (G. S.) and Spencer, Law of Electric Lighting.* New edition, crown 8vo, 12*s.* 6*d.*

*Boyesen (H. H.) Modern Vikings : Stories of Life and Sport* in Norseland. Cr. 8vo, 6*s.*

———— *Story of Norway.* Illustrated, sm. 8vo, 7*s.* 6*d.*

*Boy's Froissart. King Arthur. Knightly Legends of Wales. Percy.* See LANIER.

*Bradshaw (J.) New Zealand as it is.* 8vo, 12*s.* 6*d.*

———— *New Zealand of To-day,* 1884-87. 8vo, 14*s.*

*Brannt (W. T.) Animal and Vegetable Fats and Oils.* Illust., 8vo, 35*s.*

———— *Manufacture of Soap and Candles, with many Formulas.* Illust., 8vo, 35*s.*

———— *Manufacture of Vinegar, Cider, and Fruit Wines.* Illustrated, 8vo.

———— *Metallic Alloys. Chiefly from the German of Krupp* and Wildberger. Crown 8vo, 12*s.* 6*d.*

*Bright (John) Public Letters.* Crown 8vo, 7*s.* 6*d.*

*Brisse (Baron) Ménus (366).* A *ménu,* in French and English, for every Day in the Year. 2nd Edition. Crown 8vo, 5*s.*

*Brittany.* See BLACKBURN.

*Browne (G. Lennox) Voice Use and Stimulants.* Sm. 8vo, 3*s.* 6*d.*

———— *and Behnke (Emil) Voice, Song, and Speech.* N. ed., 5*s.*

*Brumm (C.) Bismarck, his Deeds and Aims; reply to " Bismarck* Dynasty." 8vo, 1*s.*

*Bruntie's Diary. A Tour round the World.* By C. E. B., 1*s.* 6*d.*

*Bryant (W. C.) and Gay (S. H.) History of the United States* 4 vols., royal 8vo, profusely Illustrated, 60*s.*

*Bryce (Rev. Professor) Manitoba.* Illust. Crown 8vo, 7*s.* 6*d.*

———— *Short History of the Canadian People.* 7*s.* 6*d.*

*Bulkeley (Owen T.) Lesser Antilles.* Pref. by D. MORRIS. Illus., crown 8vo, boards, 2*s.* 6*d.*

*Burnaby (Mrs. F.) High Alps in Winter; or, Mountaineering*
in Search of Health. With Illustrations, &c., 14*s*. See also MAIN.
*Burnley ( J.) History of the Silk Trade.*
—— *History of Wool and Woolcombing.* Illust. 8vo, 21*s*.
*Burton (Sir R. F.) Early, Public, and Private Life.* Edited
by F. HITCHMAN. 2 vols., 8vo, 36*s*.
*Butler (Sir W. F.) Campaign of the Cataracts.* Illust., 8vo, 18*s*.
—— *Invasion of England, told twenty years after.* 2*s*. 6*d*.
—— *Red Cloud ; or, the Solitary Sioux.* Imperial 16mo,
numerous illustrations, gilt edges, 3*s*. 6*d*.; plainer binding, 2*s*. 6*d*.
—— *The Great Lone Land ; Red River Expedition.* 7*s*. 6*d*.
—— *The Wild North Land ; the Story of a Winter Journey*
with Dogs across Northern North America. 8vo, 18*s*. Cr. 8vo, 7*s*. 6*d*.
*Bynner (E. L.) Agnes Surriage.* Crown 8vo, 10*s*. 6*d*.


*CABLE (G. W.) Bonaventure: A Prose Pastoral of Acadian*
Louisiana. Sm. post 8vo, 5*s*.
*Cadogan(Lady A.) Drawing-room Plays.* 10*s*. 6*d*. ; acting ed.,
6*d*. each.
—— *Illustrated Games of Patience.* Twenty-four Diagrams
in Colours, with Text. Fcap. 4to, 12*s*. 6*d*.
—— *New Games of Patience.* Coloured Diagrams, 4to, 12*s*.6*d*.
*Caldecott (Randolph) Memoir.* By HENRY BLACKBURN. With
170 Examples of the Artist's Work. 14*s*.; new edit., 7*s*. 6*d*.
—— *Sketches.* With an Introduction by H. BLACKBURN.
4to, picture boards, 2*s*. 6*d*.
*California.* See NORDHOFF.
*Callan (H.) Wanderings on Wheel and on Foot.* Cr. 8vo, 1*s*. 6*d*.
*Campbell (Lady Colin) Book of the Running Brook: and of*
Still Waters. 5*s*.
*Canadian People: Short History.* Crown 8vo, 7*s*. 6*d*.
*Carbutt (Mrs.) Five Months' Fine Weather in Canada,*
West U.S., and Mexico. Crown 8vo, 5*s*.
*Carleton, City Legends.* Special Edition, illus., royal 8vo,
12*s*. 6*d*. ; ordinary edition, crown 8vo, 1*s*.
—— *City Ballads.* Illustrated, 12*s*. 6*d*. New Ed. (Rose
Library), 16mo, 1*s*.
—— *Farm Ballads, Farm Festivals, and Farm Legends.*
Paper boards, 1*s*. each ; 1 vol., small post 8vo, 3*s*. 6*d*.
*Carnegie (A.) American Four-in-Hand in Britain.* Small
4to, Illustrated, 10*s* 6*d*. Popular Edition, paper, 1*s*.
—— *Round the World.* 8vo, 10*s*. 6*d*.
—— *Triumphant Democracy.* 6*s*. ; also 1*s*. 6*d*. and 1*s*.
*Chairman's Handbook.* By R. F. D. PALGRAVE. 5th Edit., 2*s*.

*Changed Cross, &c.* Religious Poems. 16mo, 2s. 6d.; calf, 6s.

*Chess.* See BIRD (H. E.).

*Children's Praises. Hymns for Sunday-Schools and Services.*
Compiled by LOUISA H. H. TRISTRAM. 4d.

*Choice Editions of Choice Books.* 2s. 6d. each. Illustrated by
C. W. COPE, R.A., T. CRESWICK, R.A., E. DUNCAN, BIRKET
FOSTER, J. C. HORSLEY, A.R.A., G. HICKS, R. REDGRAVE, R.A.,
C. STONEHOUSE, F. TAYLER, G. THOMAS, H. J. TOWNSHEND,
E. H. WEHNERT, HARRISON WEIR, &c.

| | |
|---|---|
| Bloomfield's Farmer's Boy. | Milton's L'Allegro. |
| Campbell's Pleasures of Hope. | Poetry of Nature. Harrison Weir. |
| Coleridge's Ancient Mariner. | Rogers' (Sam.) Pleasures of Memory. |
| Goldsmith's Deserted Village. | Shakespeare's Songs and Sonnets. |
| Goldsmith's Vicar of Wakefield. | Tennyson's May Queen. |
| Gray's Elegy in a Churchyard. | Elizabethan Poets. |
| Keats' Eve of St. Agnes. | Wordsworth's Pastoral Poems. |

" Such works are a glorious beatification for a poet."—*Athenæum.*

*Christ in Song.* By PHILIP SCHAFF. New Ed., gilt edges, 6s.

*Chromo-Lithography.* See AUDSLEY.

*Cicero, Tusculan Disputation, I. (Death no bane).* Translated
by R. BLACK. Small crown 8vo.

*Clarke (H. P.)* See WILLS.

*Clarke (P.) Three Diggers: a Tale of the Australian Fifties.*
Crown 8vo, 6s.

*Cochran (W.) Pen and Pencil in Asia Minor.* Illust., 8vo, 21s.

*Collingwood (Harry) Under the Meteor Flag.* The Log of a
Midshipman. Illustrated, small post 8vo, gilt, 3s. 6d.; plainer, 2s. 6d.

—— *Voyage of the " Aurora."* Gilt, 3s. 6d.; plainer, 2s. 6d.

*Collinson (Sir R.; Adm.) H.M.S. "Enterprise" in search of Sir*
J. Franklin. 8vo.

*Colonial Year-book.* Edited and compiled by A. J. R.
TRENDELL. Crown 8vo, 6s.

*Cook (Dutton) Book of the Play.* New Edition. 1 vol., 3s. 6d.

—— *On the Stage: Studies.* 2 vols., 8vo, cloth, 24s.

*Cozzens (F.) American Yachts.* 27 Plates, 22 × 28 inches.
Proofs, £21; Artist's Proofs, £31 10s.

*Craddock (C. E.) Despot of Broomsedge Cove.* Crown 8vo, 6s.

*Crew (B. J.) Practical Treatise on Petroleum.* Illust., 8vo, 28s.

*Crouch (A.P.) Glimpses of Feverland: a Cruise in West African*
Waters. Crown 8vo, 6s.

—— *On a Surf-bound Coast.* Crown 8vo, 7s. 6d.

*Cumberland(Stuart) Thought Reader's Thoughts.* Cr. 8vo., 10s.6d.

—— *Queen's Highway from Ocean to Ocean.* Ill., 8vo, 18s.;
new ed., 7s. 6d.

---

*Cumberland (S.) Vasty deep : a Strange Story of To-day.* New Edition, 6s.

*Cundall (Joseph).* See " Remarkable Bindings."

*Cushing (W.) Initials and Pseudonyms.* Large 8vo, 25s.; second series, large 8vo, 21s.

*Custer (Eliz. B.) Tenting on the Plains; Gen. Custer in Kansas and Texas.* Royal 8vo, 18s.

*Cutcliffe (H. C.) Trout Fishing in Rapid Streams.* Cr. 8vo, 3s. 6d.

*DALY (Mrs. D.) Digging, Squatting, and Pioneering in* Northern South Australia. 8vo, 12s.

*D'Anvers. Elementary History of Art.* New ed., 360 illus., 2 vols., cr. 8vo. I. Architecture, &c., 5s.; II. Painting, 6s.; 1 vol., 10s. 6d.

—— *Elementary History of Music.* Crown 8vo, 2s. 6d.

*Davis (Clement) Modern Whist.* 4s.

—— *(C. T.) Bricks, Tiles, Terra-Cotta, &c.* N. ed. 8vo, 25s.

—— *Manufacture of Leather.* With many Illustrations. 52s.6d.

—— *Manufacture of Paper.* 28s.

—— *(G. B.) Outlines of International Law.* 8vo. 10s. 6d.

*Dawidowsky. Glue, Gelatine, Isinglass, Cements,&c.* 8vo, 12s.6d.

*Day of My Life at Eton.* By an ETON BOY. New ed. 16mo, 1s.

*Day's Collacon : an Encyclopædia of Prose Quotations.* Imperial 8vo, cloth, 31s. 6d.

*De Leon (E.) Under the Stars and under the Crescent.* N.ed.,6s.

*Dethroning Shakspere. Letters to the Daily Telegraph ; and* Editorial Papers. Crown 8vo, 2s. 6d.

*Dickinson (Charles M.) The Children, and other Verses.* Sm. 8vo, gilt edges, 5s.

*Dictionary.* See TOLHAUSEN, " Technological."

*Diggle (J. W, ; Canon) Lancashire Life of Bishop Fraser.* 8vo, 12s. 6d.

*Donnelly (Ignatius) Atlantis ; or, the Antediluvian World.* 7th Edition, crown 8vo, 12s. 6d.

—— *Ragnarok : The Age of Fire and Gravel.* Illustrated, crown 8vo, 12s. 6d.

—— *The Great Cryptogram : Francis Bacon's Cipher in the* so-called Shakspere Plays. With facsimiles. 2 vols., 30s.

*Donkin (J. G.) Trooper and Redskin : N.W. Mounted Police,* Canada. Crown 8vo, 8s. 6d.

*Dougall (James Dalziel) Shooting: its Appliances, Practice,* and Purpose. New Edition, revised with additions. Crown 8vo, 7s. 6d.
"The book is admirable in every way. . . . . We wish it every success."—*Globe.*
"A very complete treatise. . . . . Likely to take high rank as an authority on shooting."—*Daily News.*

*Doughty (H.M.) Friesland Meres, and through the Netherlands*
Illustrated, crown 8vo, 8s. 6d.

*Dramatic Year: Brief Criticisms of Events in the U.S.* By W.
ARCHER. Crown 8vo, 6s.

*Dunstan Standard Readers.* Ed. by A. GILL, of Cheltenham.

*EARL (H. P.) Randall Trevor.* 2 vols., crown 8vo, 21s.

*Eastwood (F.) In Satan's Bonds.* 2 vols., crown 8vo, 21s.

*Edmonds (C.) Poetry of the Anti-Jacobin. With Additional*
matter. New ed. Illust., crown 8vo, 7s. 6d. ; large paper, 21s.

*Educational List and Directory for* 1887-88. 5s.

*Educational Works* published in Great Britain. A Classi-
fied Catalogue. Third Edition, 8vo, cloth extra, 6s.

*Edwards (E.) American Steam Engineer.* Illust., 12mo, 12s. 6d.

*Eight Months on the Argentine Gran Chaco.* 8vo, 8s. 6d.

*Elliott (H. W.) An Arctic Province : Alaska and the Seal*
Islands. Illustrated from Drawings ; also with Maps. 16s.

*Emerson (Dr. P. H.) English Idylls.* Small post 8vo, 2s.

—— *Pictures of East Anglian Life.* Ordinary edit., 105s. ;
édit. de luxe, 17 × 13½, vellum, morocco back, 147s.

—— *Naturalistic Photography for Art Students.* Illustrated.
New edit. 5s.

—— *and Goodall. Life and Landscape on the Norfolk*
Broads. Plates 12 × 8 inches, 126s.; large paper, 210s.

*Emerson in Concord: A Memoir written by Edward Waldo*
EMERSON. 8vo, 7s. 6d.

*English Catalogue of Books.* Vol. III., 1872—1880. Royal
8vo, half-morocco, 42s. See also " Index."

*English Etchings.* Published Quarterly. 3s. 6d. Vol. VI., 25s.

*English Philosophers.* Edited by E. B. IVAN MÜLLER, M.A.
Crown 8vo volumes of 180 or 200 pp., price 3s. 6d. each.

Francis Bacon, by Thomas Fowler. | Shaftesbury and Hutcheson.
Hamilton, by W. H. S. Monck. | Adam Smith, by J. A. Farrer.
Hartley and James Mill. |

*Esmarch (F.) Handbook of Surgery.* Translation from the
last German Edition. With 647 new Illustrations. 8vo, leather, 24s.

*Eton. About some Fellows.* New Edition, 1s.

*Evelyn. Life of Mrs. Godolphin.* By WILLIAM HARCOURT,
of Nuneham Steel Portrait. Extra binding, gilt top, 7s. 6d.

*Eves (C. W.) West Indies.* (Royal Colonial Institute publica-
tion.) Crown 8vo, 7s. 6d.

*FARINI (G. A.) Through the Kalahari Desert.* 8vo, 21s.

*Farm Ballads, Festivals, and Legends.* See CARLETON.

*Fay (T.) Three Germanys ; glimpses into their History.* 2 vols., 8vo, 35*s.*

*Fenn (G. Manville) Off to the Wilds: a Story for Boys.* Profusely Illustrated. Crown 8vo, gilt edges, 3*s.* 6*d.*; plainer, 2*s.* 6*d.*

———— *Silver Cañon.* Illust., gilt ed., 3*s.* 6*d.* ; plainer, 2*s.* 6*d.*

*Fennell (Greville) Book of the Roach.* New Edition, 12mo, 2*s.*

*Ferns.* See HEATH.

*Fitzgerald (P.) Book Fancier.* Cr. 8vo. 5*s.* ; large pap. 12*s.* 6*d.*

*Fleming (Sandford) England and Canada : a Tour.* Cr. 8vo, 6*s.*

*Florence.* See YRIARTE.

*Folkard (R., Jun.) Plant Lore, Legends, and Lyrics.* 8vo, 16*s.*

*Forbes (H. O.) Naturalist in the Eastern Archipelago.* 8vo. 21*s.*

*Foreign Countries and British Colonies.* Cr. 8vo, 3*s.* 6*d.* each.

| | |
|---|---|
| Australia, by J. F. Vesey Fitzgerald. | Japan, by S. Mossman. |
| Austria, by D. Kay, F.R.G.S. | Peru, by Clements R. Markham. |
| Denmark and Iceland, by E. C. Otté. | Russia, by W. R. Morfill, M.A. |
| Egypt, by S. Lane Poole, B.A. | Spain, by Rev. Wentworth Webster. |
| France, by Miss M. Roberts. | Sweden and Norway, by Woods. |
| Germany, by S. Baring-Gould. | ,West Indies, by C. H. Eden, |
| Greece, by L. Sergeant, B.A. | F.R.G.S. |

*Franc (Maud Jeanne).* Small post 8vo, uniform, gilt edges :—

| | |
|---|---|
| Emily's Choice. 5*s.* | Vermont Vale. 5*s.* |
| Hall's Vineyard. 4*s.* | Minnie's Mission. 4*s.* |
| John's Wife : A Story of Life in South Australia. 4*s.* | Little Mercy. 4*s.* |
| | Beatrice Melton's Discipline. 4*s.* |
| Marian ; or, The Light of Some One's Home. 5*s.* | No Longer a Child. 4*s.* |
| | Golden Gifts. 4*s.* |
| Silken Cords and Iron Fetters. 4*s.* | Two Sides to Every Question. 4*s.* |
| Into the Light. 4*s.* | Master of Ralston. 4*s.* |

\*\*\* There is also a re-issue in cheaper form at 2*s.* 6*l.* per vol.

*Frank's Ranche ; or, My Holiday in the Rockies.* A Contribution to the Inquiry into What we are to Do with our Boys. 5*s.*

*Fraser (Bishop).* See DIGGLE.

*French.* See JULIEN and PORCHER.

*Fresh Woods and Pastures New.* By the Author of " An Amateur Angler's Days." 1*s.* 6*d.*; large paper, 5*s.* ; new ed., 1*s.*

*Froissart.* See LANIER.

*Fuller (Edward) Fellow Travellers.* 3*s.* 6*d.*

———— See also " Dramatic Year."

*GASPARIN (Countess A. de) Sunny Fields and Shady Woods.* 6*s.*

*Geary (Grattan) Burma after the Conquest.* 7*s.* 6*d.*

*Geffcken (F. H.) British Empire.* Translated by S. J. MAC-MULLAN. Crown 8vo, 7*s.* 6*d.*

*Gentle Life* (Queen Edition). 2 vols. in 1, small 4to, 6s.

## THE GENTLE LIFE SERIES.

Price 6s. each ; or in calf extra, price 10s. 6d. ; Smaller Edition, cloth
extra, 2s. 6d., except where price is named.

*The Gentle Life.* Essays in aid of the Formation of Character.
*About in the World.* Essays by Author of "The Gentle Life."
*Like unto Christ.* New Translation of Thomas à Kempis.
*Familiar Words.* A Quotation Handbook. 6s.; n. ed. 3s.6d.
*Essays by Montaigne.* Edited by the Author of "The Gentle
Life."
*The Gentle Life.* 2nd Series.
*The Silent Hour: Essays, Original and Selected.*
*Half-Length Portraits.* Short Studies of Notable Persons.
By J. HAIN FRISWELL.
*Essays on English Writers,* for Students in English Literature.
*Other People's Windows.* By J. HAIN FRISWELL. 6s. ; new
ed., 3s. 6d.
*A Man's Thoughts.* By J. HAIN FRISWELL.
*Countess of Pembroke's Arcadia.* By Sir P. SIDNEY. 6s.; new
ed., 3s. 6d.

---

*Germany.* By S. BARING-GOULD. Crown 8vo, 3s. 6d.
*Gibbon* (*C.*) *Beyond Compare : a Story.* 3 vols., cr. 8vo, 31s. 6d.
*Giles* (*E.*) *Australia twice Traversed : five Expeditions,* 1872-76.
With Maps and Illust. 2 vols, 8vo, 30s.
*Gillespie* (*W. M.*) *Surveying.* Revised and enlarged by CADEY
STALEY. 8vo, 21s.
*Goethe. Faustus.* Translated in the original rhyme and metre
by A. H. HUTH. Crown 8vo, 5s.
*Goldsmith. She Stoops to Conquer.* Introduction by AUSTIN
DOBSON ; the designs by E. A. ABBEY. Imperial 4to, 42s.
*Gordon* (*J. E. H., B.A. Cantab.*) *Electric Lighting.* Ill. 8vo,18s.
——— *Physical Treatise on Electricity and Magnetism.* 2nd
Edition, enlarged, with coloured, full-page, &c., Illust. 2 vols., 8vo, 42s.
——— *Electricity for Schools.* Illustrated. Crown 8vo, 5s.
*Gouffé* (*Jules*) *Royal Cookery Book.* New Edition, with plates
in colours, Woodcuts, &c., 8vo, gilt edges, 42s.
——— Domestic Edition, half-bound, 10s. 6d.
*Grant* (*General, U.S.*) *Personal Memoirs.* With Illustrations
Maps, &c. 2 vols., 8vo, 28s.
*Great Artists.* See "Biographies."

*Great Musicians.* Edited by F. HJEFFER. A Series of
Biographies, crown 8vo, 3s. each :—

| | | |
|---|---|---|
| Bach. | Handel. | Rossini. |
| Beethoven. | Haydn. | Schubert. |
| Berlioz. | Mendelssohn. | Schumann. |
| English Church Com- | Mozart. | Richard Wagner. |
| posers. By BARRETT. | Purcell. | Weber. |

*Groves (J. Percy) Charmouth Grange.* Gilt, 5s.; plainer, 2s. 6d.

*Guizot's History of France.* Translated by R. BLACK. In
8 vols., super-royal 8vo, cloth extra, gilt, each 24s. In cheaper
binding, 8 vols., at 10s. 6d. each.
"It supplies a want which has long been felt, and ought to be in the hands of all
students of history."—*Times.*

————————— *Masson's School Edition.* Abridged
from the Translation by Robert Black, with Chronological Index, His-
torical and Genealogical Tables, &c. By Professor GUSTAVE MASSON,
B.A. With Portraits, Illustrations, &c. 1 vol., 8vo, 600 pp., 5s.

*Guyon (Mde.) Life.* By UPHAM. 6th Edition, crown 8vo, 6s.

*HALFORD (F. M.) Floating Flies, and how to Dress them.*
New edit., with Coloured plates. 8vo, 15s.

————————— *Dry Fly-Fishing, Theory and Practice.* Col. Plates, 25s.

*Hall (W. W.) How to Live Long; or,* 1408 *Maxims.* 2s.

*Hamilton (E.) Fly-fishing for Salmon, Trout, and Grayling ;*
their Habits, Haunts, and History. Illust., 6s.; large paper, 10s. 6d.

*Hands (T.) Numerical Exercises in Chemistry.* Cr. 8vo, 2s. 6d.
and 2s.; Answers separately, 6d.

*Hardy (A. S.) Passe-rose : a Romance.* Crown 8vo, 6s.

*Hardy (Thomas).* See "Low's Standard Novels."

*Hare (J. L. Clark) American Constitutional Law.* 2 vls. 8vo, 63s.

*Harper's Magazine.* Monthly. 160 pages, fully illustrated, 1s.
Vols., half yearly, I.—XVIII., super-royal 8vo, 8s. 6d. each.
"'Harper's Magazine' is so thickly sown with excellent illustrations that to coun
them would be a work of time ; not that it is a picture magazine, for the engravings
illustrate the text after the manner seen in some of our choicest *éditions de luxe.*"—
*St. James's Gazette.*
"It is so pretty, so big, and so cheap. . . . An extraordinary shillingsworth—
160 large octavo pages, with over a score of articles, and more than three times as
many illustrations."—*Edinburgh Daily Review.*
"An amazing shillingsworth . . . combining choice literature of both nations."—
*Nonconformist.*

*Harper's Young People.* Vols. I.-V., profusely Illustrated
with woodcuts and coloured plates. Royal 4to, extra binding, each
7s. 6d.; gilt edges, 8s. Published Weekly, in wrapper, 1d.; Annual
Subscription, post free, 6s. 6d.; Monthly, in wrapper, with coloured
plate, 6d.; Annual Subscription, post free, 7s. 6d.

*Harris (Bishop of Michigan) Dignity of Man : Select Sermons.*
Crown 8vo, 8s. 6d.

*Harris (W. B.) Land of African Sultan : Travels in Morocco.*
Illust., crown 8vo, 10s. 6d.; large paper, 31s. 6d.

*Harrison (Mary) Complete Cookery Book.* Crown 8vo.
—— *Skilful Cook.* New edition, crown 8vo, 5*s.*
*Harrison (W.) Memorable London Houses : a Guide.* Illust.
New edition, 18mo, 1*s.* 6*d.*
*Hatton (Joseph) Journalistic London : with Engravings and*
Portraits of Distinguished Writers of the Day. Fcap. 4to, 12*s.* 6*d.*
—— See also LOW'S STANDARD NOVELS.
*Haweis (Mrs.) Art of Housekeeping : a Bridal Garland.* 2*s.*6*d.*
*Hawthorne (Nathaniel) Life.* By JOHN R. LOWELL.
*Heldmann (B.) Mutiny of the Ship " Leander."* Gilt edges,
3*s.* 6*d.;* plainer, 2*s.* 6*d.*
*Henty. Winning his Spurs.* Cr. 8vo, 3*s.* 6*d.* ; plainer, 2*s.* 6*d.*
—— *Cornet of Horse.* Cr. 8vo, 3*s.* 6*d.*; plainer, 2*s.* 6*d.*
—— *Jack Archer.* Illust. 3*s.* 6*d.* ; plainer, 2*s.* 6*d.*
*Henty (Richmond) Australiana : My Early Life.* 5*s.*
*Herrick (Robert) Poetry.* Preface by AUSTIN DOBSON. With
numerous Illustrations by E. A. ABBEY. 4to, gilt edges, 42*s.*
*Hetley (Mrs. E.) Native Flowers of New Zealand.* Chromos
from Drawings. Three Parts, 63*s.*; extra binding, 73*s.* 6*d.*
*Hicks (E. S.) Our Boys: How to Enter the Merchant Service.* 5*s.*
—— *Yachts, Boats and Canoes.* Illustrated. 8vo, 10*s.* 6*d.*
*Hinman (R.) Eclectic Physical Geography.* Crown 8vo, 5*s.*
*Hitchman. Public Life of the Earl of Beaconsfield.* 3*s.* 6*d.*
*Hoey (Mrs. Cashel)* See LOW'S STANDARD NOVELS.
*Holder (C. F.) Marvels of Animal Life.* Illustrated. 8*s.* 6*d.*
—— *Ivory King: Elephant and Allies.* Illustrated. 8*s.* 6*d.*
—— *Living Lights : Phosphorescent Animals and Vegetables.*
Illustrated. 8vo, 8*s.* 6*d.*
*Holmes (O. W.) Before the Curfew, &c. Occasional Poems.* 5*s.*
—— *Last Leaf : a Holiday Volume.* 42*s.*
—— *Mortal Antipathy*, 8*s.* 6*d.* ; also 2*s.* ; paper, 1*s.*
—— *Our Hundred Days in Europe.* 6*s.* Large Paper, 15*s.*
—— *Poetical Works.* 2 vols., 18mo, gilt tops, 10*s.* 6*d.*
—— See also " Rose Library."
*Howard (Blanche Willis) Open Door.* Crown 8vo, 6*s.*
*Howorth (H. H.) Mammoth and the Flood.* 8vo, 18*s.*
*Hugo (V.) Notre Dame.* With coloured etchings and 150
engravings. 2 vols.. 8\o, vellum cloth, 30*s.*
*Hundred Greatest Men (The).* 8 portfolios, 21*s.* each, or 4 vols.,
half-morocco, gilt edges, 10 guineas. New Ed., 1 vol., royal 8vo, 21*s.*
*Hymnal Companion to the Book of Common Prayer.* By
BISHOP BICKERSTETH. In various styles and bindings from 1*d.* to
31*s.* 6*d. Price List and Prospectus will be forwarded on application.*

*ILLUSTRATED Text-Books of Art-Education.* Edited by EDWARD J. POYNTER, R.A. Illustrated, and strongly bound, 5*s*. Now ready :—

PAINTING.

Classic and Italian. By HEAD. | French and Spanish. German, Flemish, and Dutch. | English and American.

ARCHITECTURE.

Classic and Early Christian. Gothic and Renaissance. By T. ROGER SMITH.

SCULPTURE.

Antique : Egyptian and Greek. Renaissance and Modern. By LEADER SCOTT.

*Inderwick (F. A. ; Q.C.) Side Lights on the Stuarts. Essays.* Illustrated, 8vo, 18*s*.

*Index to the English Catalogue, Jan.,* 1874, *to Dec.,* 1880. Royal 8vo, half-morocco, 18*s*.

*Inglis (Hon. James ; " Maori ") Our New Zealand Cousins.* Small post 8vo, 6*s*.

—— *Tent Life in Tiger Land : Twelve Years a Pioneer* Planter. Col. plates, roy. 8vo, 18*s*.

*Irving (Washington).* Library Edition of his Works in 27 vols., Copyright, with the Author's Latest Revisions. " Geoffrey Crayon " Edition, large square 8vo. 12*s*. 6*d*. per vol. *See also* "Little Britain."

*JACKSON. New Style Vertical Writing Copy-Books* Series I, Nos. I.—XII., 2*d*. and 1*d*. each.

—— *New Series of Vertical Writing Copy-books.* 22 Nos.

—— *Shorthand of Arithmetic : a Companion to all Arithmetics.* Crown 8vo, 1*s*. 6*d*.

*Japan.* See ANDERSON, ARTISTIC, AUDSLEY, also MORSE.

*Jerdon (Gertrude) Key-hole Country.* Illustrated. Crown 8vo, cloth, 2*s*.

*Johnston (H. H.) River Congo, from its Mouth to Bolobo.* New Edition, 8vo, 21*s*.

*Johnstone (D. Lawson) Land of the Mountain Kingdom.* Illust., crown 8vo. 5*s*.

*Julien (F.) English Student's French Examiner.* 16mo, 2*s*.

—— *Conversational French Reader.* 16mo, cloth, 2*s*. 6*d*.

——*French at Home and at School.* Book I., Accidence. 2*s*.

—— *First Lessons in Conversational French Grammar.* 1*s*.

—— *Petites Leçons de Conversation et de Grammaire.* 3*s*.

—— *Phrases of Daily Use.* Limp cloth, 6*d*.

*KARR (H. W. Seton) Shores and Alps of Alaska.* 8vo, 16*s*.

*Keats. Endymion.* Illust. by W. ST. JOHN HARPER. Imp. 4to, gilt top, 42*s*.

*Kempis (Thomas à) Daily Text-Book.* Square 16mo, 2s. 6d. ;
interleaved as a Birthday Book, 3s. 6d.

*Kennedy (E. B.) Blacks and Bushrangers, adventures in North*
Queensland. Illust., crown 8vo, 7s. 6.t.

*Kent's Commentaries : an Abridgment for Students of American*
Law. By EDEN F. THOMPSON. 10s. 6d.

*Kerr (W. M.) Far Interior : Cape of Good Hope, across the*
Zambesi, to the Lake Regions. Illustrated from Sketches, 2 vols.
8vo, 32s.

*Kershaw (S. W.) Protestants from France in their English*
Home. Crown 8vo, 6s.

*King (Henry) Savage London; Riverside Characters, &c.*
Crown 8vo, 6s.

*Kingston (W. H. G.) Works.* Illustrated, 16mo, gilt edges,
3s. 6d. ; plainer binding, plain edges, 2s. 6d. each.

| | |
|---|---|
| Ben Burton. | Heir of Kilfinnan. |
| Captain Mugford, or, Our Salt and Fresh Water Tutors. | Snow-Shoes and Canoes. |
| | Two Supercargoes. |
| Dick Cheveley. | With Axe and Rifle. |

*Kingsley (Rose) Children of Westminster Abbey : Studies in*
English History. 5s.

*Knight (E. J.) Cruise of the "Falcon."* New Ed. Cr. 8vo,
7s. 6d.

*Knox (Col.) Boy Travellers on the Congo.* Illus. Cr. 8vo, 7s. 6d.

*Kunhardt (C. B.) Small Yachts : Design and Construction.* 35s.

—— *Steam Yachts and Launches.* Illustrated. 4to, 16s.


*L*ANGLEY (S. P.) New Astronomy. Ill. Cr. 8vo. 10s. 6d.

*Lanier's Works.* Illustrated, crown 8vo, gilt edges, 7s. 6d.
each.

| | |
|---|---|
| Boy's King Arthur. | Boy's Percy: Ballads of Love and |
| Boy's Froissart. | Adventure, selected from the |
| Boy's Knightly Legends of Wales. | "Reliques." |

*Lansdell (H.) Through Siberia.* 2 vols., 8vo, 30s.; 1 vol., 10s. 6d.

—— *Russia in Central Asia.* Illustrated. 2 vols., 42s.

—— *Through Central Asia; Russo-Afghan Frontier, &c.*
8vo, 12s.

*Larden (W.) School Course on Heat.* Third Ed., Illust. 5s.

*Laurie (A.) Conquest of the Moon : a Story of the Bayouda.*
Illust., crown 8vo, 7s. 6d.

*Layard (Mrs. Granville) Through the West Indies.* Small
post 8vo, 2s. 6d.

*Lea (H. C.). History of the Inquisition of the Middle Ages.*
3 vols., 8vo, 42s.

*Lemon (M.) Small House over the Water, and Stories.* Illust.
by Cruikshank, &c. Crown 8vo, 6s.

*Leo XIII. : Life.* By BERNARD O'REILLY. With Steel
Portrait from Photograph, &c. Large 8vo, 18s.; *édit. de luxe*, 63s.

*Leonardo da Vinci's Literary Works.* Edited by Dr. JEAN
PAUL RICHTER. Containing his Writings on Painting, Sculpture,
and Architecture, his Philosophical Maxims, Humorous Writings, and
Miscellaneous Notes on Personal Events, on his Contemporaries, on
Literature, &c. ; published from Manuscripts. 2 vols., imperial 8vo,
containing about 200 Drawings in Autotype Reproductions, and numerous other Illustrations. Twelve Guineas.

*Library of Religious Poetry.* Best Poems of all Ages. Edited
by SCHAFF and GILMAN. Royal 8vo, 21s.; cheaper binding, 10s. 6d.

*Lindsay (W. S.) History of Merchant Shipping.* Over 150
Illustrations, Maps, and Charts. In 4 vols., demy 8vo, cloth extra.
Vols. 1 and 2, 11s. each ; vols. 3 and 4, 14s. each. 4 vols., 50s.

*Little (Archibald J.) Through the Yang-tse Gorges : Trade and*
. Travel in Western China. New Edition. 8vo, 10s. 6d.

*Little Britain, The Spectre Bridegroom,* and *Legend of Sleepy*
Hollow. By WASHINGTON IRVING. An entirely New *Édition de
luxe*. Illustrated by 120 very fine Engravings on Wood, by Mr.
J. D. COOPER. Designed by Mr. CHARLES O. MURRAY. Re-issue,
square crown 8vo, cloth, 6s.

*Lodge (Henry Cabot) George Washington. (American Statesmen.)*
2 vols., 12s.

*Longfellow. Maidenhood.* With Coloured Plates. Oblong
4to, 2s. 6d.; gilt edges, 3s. 6d.

—— *Courtship of Miles Standish.* Illust. by BROUGHTON,
&c. Imp. 4to, 21s.

—— *Nuremberg.* 28 Photogravures. Illum. by M. and A.
COMEGYS. 4to, 31s. 6d.

*Lowell (J. R.) Vision of Sir Launfal.* Illustrated, royal 4to, 63s.

—— *Life of Nathaniel Hawthorne.* Sm post 8vo. [*In prep.*

*Low's Standard Library of Travel and Adventure.* Crown 8vo,
uniform in cloth extra, 7s. 6d., except where price is given.
1. The Great Lone Land. By Major W. F. BUTLER, C.B.
2. The Wild North Land. By Major W. F. BUTLER, C.B.
3. How I found Livingstone. By H. M. STANLEY.
4. Through the Dark Continent. By H. M. STANLEY. 12s. 6d.
5. The Threshold of the Unknown Region. By C. R. MARK-
HAM. (4th Edition, with Additional Chapters, 10s. 6d.)
6. Cruise of the Challenger. By W. J. J. SPRY, R.N.
7. Burnaby's On Horseback through Asia Minor. 10s. 6d.
8. Schweinfurth's Heart of Africa. 2 vols., 15s.
9. Through America. By W. G. MARSHALL.
10. Through Siberia. II. and unabridged, 10s.6d. By H. LANSDELL.
11. From Home to Home. By STAVELEY HILL.
12. Cruise of the Falcon. By E. J. KNIGHT.

*Low's Standard Library, &c.—continued.*
13. Through Masai Land. By JOSEPH THOMSON.
14. To the Central African Lakes. By JOSEPH THOMSON.
15. Queen's Highway. By STUART CUMBERLAND.

*Low's Standard Novels.* Small post 8vo, cloth extra, 6s. each, unless otherwise stated

JAMES BAKER. John Westacott.

WILLIAM BLACK.
A Daughter of Heth.—House-Boat.—In Far Lochaber.—In Silk Attire.—Kilmeny.—Lady Silverdale's Sweetheart.—Sunrise.—Three Feathers.

R. D. BLACKMORE.
Alice Lorraine.—Christowell, a Dartmoor Tale.—Clara Vaughan.—Cradock Nowell.—Cripps the Carrier.—Erema; or, My Father's Sin.—Lorna Doone.—Mary Anerley.—Tommy Upmore.

G. W. CABLE. Bonaventure. 5s.

Miss COLERIDGE. An English Squire.

C. E. CRADDOCK. Despot of Broomsedge Cove.

Mrs. B. M. CROKER. Some One Else.

STUART CUMBERLAND. Vasty Deep.

E. DE LEON. Under the Stars and Crescent.

Miss BETHAM-EDWARDS. Halfway.

Rev. E. GILLIAT, M.A. Story of the Dragonnades.

THOMAS HARDY.
A Laodicean.—Far from the Madding Crowd.—Mayor of Casterbridge.—Pair of Blue Eyes.—Return of the Native.—The Hand of Ethelberta.—The Trumpet Major.—Two on a Tower.

JOSEPH HATTON. Old House at Sandwich.—Three Recruits.

Mrs. CASHEL HOEY.
A Golden Sorrow.—A Stern Chase.—Out of Court.

BLANCHE WILLIS HOWARD. Open Door.

JEAN INGELOW.
Don John.—John Jerome (5s.).—Sarah de Berenger.

GEORGE MAC DONALD.
Adela Cathcart.—Guild Court.—Mary Marston.—Stephen Archer (New Ed. of "Gifts").—The Vicar's Daughter.—Orts.—Weighed and Wanting.

Mrs. MACQUOID. Diane.—Elinor Dryden.

HELEN MATHERS. My Lady Greensleeves.

DUFFIELD OSBORNE. Spell of Ashtaroth (5s.)

Mrs. J. H. RIDDELL.
Alaric Spenceley.—Daisies and Buttercups.—The Senior Partner.—A Struggle for Fame.

W. CLARK RUSSELL.
Frozen Pirate.—Jack's Courtship.—John Holdsworth.—A Sailor's Sweetheart.—Sea Queen.—Watch Below.—Strange Voyage.—Wreck of the Grosvenor.—The Lady Maud.—Little Loo.

B

*Low's Standard Novels—continued.*
FRANK R. STOCKTON.
  Bee-man of Orn.—The Late Mrs. Null.—Hundredth Man.
Mrs. HARRIET B. STOWE.
  My Wife and I.—Old Town Folk.—We and our Neighbours.—
  Poganuc People, their Loves and Lives.
JOSEPH THOMSON.  Ulu: an African Romance.
LEW. WALLACE.  Ben Hur: a Tale of the Christ.
CONSTANCE FENIMORE WOOLSON.
  Anne.—East Angels.—For the Major (5s.).
  French Heiress in her own Chateau.
        See also SEA STORIES.

*Low's Standard Novels.*  NEW ISSUE at short intervals.  Cr.
8vo, 2s. 6d.; fancy boards, 2s.
BLACKMORE.
  Clara Vaughan.—Cripps the Carrier.—Lorna Doone.—Mary
  Anerley.
HARDY.
  Madding Crowd.—Mayor of Casterbridge.—Trumpet-Major.
HATTON.  Three Recruits.
HOLMES.  Guardian Angel.
MAC DONALD.  Adela Cathcart.—Guild Court.
RIDDELL.  Daisies and Buttercups.—Senior Partner.
STOCKTON.  Casting Away of Mrs. Lecks.
STOWE.  Dred.
WALFORD.  Her Great Idea.
    *To be followed immediately by*
BLACKMORE.  Alice Lorraine.—Tommy Upmore.
CABLE.  Bonaventure.
CROKER.  Some One Else.
DE LEON.  Under the Stars.
EDWARDS.  Half-Way.
HARDY.
  Hand of Ethelberta.—Pair of Blue Eyes.—Two on a Tower.
HATTON.  Old House at Sandwich.
HOEY.  Golden Sorrow.—Out of Court.—Stern Chase.
INGELOW.  John Jerome.—Sarah de Berenger.
MAC DONALD.  Vicar's Daughter.—Stephen Archer.
OLIPHANT.  Innocent.
STOCKTON.  Bee-Man of Orn.
STOWE.  Old Town Folk.—Poganuc People.
THOMSON.  Ulu.

*Low's Standard Books for Boys.*  With numerous Illustrations,
2s. 6d.; gilt edges, 3s. 6d. each.
  Dick Cheveley.  By W. H. G. KINGSTON.
  Heir of Kilfinnan.  By W. H. G. KINGSTON.
  Off to the Wilds.  By G. MANVILLE FENN.
  The Two Supercargoes.  By W. H. G. KINGSTON.
  The Silver Cañon.  By G. MANVILLE FENN.
  Under the Meteor Flag.  By HARRY COLLINGWOOD.
  Jack Archer: a Tale of the Crimea.  By G. A. HENTY.

## *Low's Standard Books for Boys—continued.*
The Mutiny on Board the Ship Leander. By B. HELDMANN.
With Axe and Rifle on the Western Prairies. By W. H. G.
KINGSTON.
Red Cloud, the Solitary Sioux : a Tale of the Great Prairie.
By Col. Sir WM. BUTLER, K.C.B.
The Voyage of the Aurora. By HARRY COLLINGWOOD.
Charmouth Grange : a Tale of the 17th Century. By J.
PERCY GROVES.
Snowshoes and Canoes. By W. H. G. KINGSTON.
The Son of the Constable of France. By LOUIS ROUSSELET.
Captain Mugford; or, Our Salt and Fresh Water Tutors.
Edited by W. H. G. KINGSTON.
The Cornet of Horse, a Tale of Marlborough's Wars. By
G. A. HENTY.
The Adventures of Captain Mago. By LEON CAHUN.
Noble Words and Noble Needs.
The King of the Tigers. By ROUSSELET.
Hans Brinker; or, The Silver Skates. By Mrs. DODGE.
The Drummer-Boy, a Story of the time of Washington. By
ROUSSELET.
Adventures in New Guinea : The Narrative of Louis Tregance.
The Crusoes of Guiana. By BOUSSENARD.
The Gold Seekers. A Sequel to the Above. By BOUSSENARD.
Winning His Spurs, a Tale of the Crusades. By G. A. HENTY.
The Blue Banner. By LEON CAHUN.

### *New Volumes for* 1889.
Startling Exploits of the Doctor. CÉLIÈRE.
Brothers Rantzau. ERCKMANN-CHATRIAN.
Young Naturalist. BIART.
Ben Burton; or, Born and Bred at Sea. KINGSTON.
Great Hunting Grounds of the World. MEUNIER.
Ran Away from the Dutch. PERELAER.
My Kalulu, Prince, King, and Slave. STANLEY.

## *Low's Standard Series of Books by Popular Writers.* Sm. cr.
8vo, cloth gilt, 2s.; gilt edges, 2s. 6d. each.
Aunt Jo's Scrap Bag. By Miss ALCOTT.
Shawl Straps. By Miss ALCOTT.
Little Men. By Miss ALCOTT.
Hitherto. By Mrs. WHITNEY.
Forecastle to Cabin. By SAMUELS. Illustrated.
In My Indian Garden. By PHIL ROBINSON.
Little Women and Little Women Wedded. By Miss ALCOTT.
Eric and Ethel. By FRANCIS FRANCIS. Illust.
Keyhole Country. By GERTRUDE JERDON. Illust.
We Girls. By Mrs. WHITNEY.
The Other Girls. A Sequel to "We Girls." By Mrs. WHITNEY.
Adventures of Jimmy Brown. Illust. By W. L. ALDEN.
Under the Lilacs. By Miss ALCOTT. Illust.
Jimmy's Cruise. By Miss ALCOTT.
Under the Punkah. By PHIL ROBINSON.

*Low's Standard Series of Books by Popular Writers—continued.*
An Old-Fashioned Girl. By Miss ALCOTT.
A Rose in Bloom. By Miss ALCOTT.
Eight Cousins. Illust. By Miss ALCOTT.
Jack and Jill. By Miss ALCOTT.
Lulu's Library. Illust. By Miss ALCOTT.
Silver Pitchers. By Miss ALCOTT.                         ,
Work and Beginning Again. Illust. By Miss ALCOTT.
A Summer in Leslie Goldthwaite's Life. By Mrs. WHITNEY.
Faith Gartney's Girlhood. By Mrs. WHITNEY.
Real Folks. By Mrs. WHITNEY.
Dred. By Mrs. STOWE.
My Wife and I. By Mrs. STOWE.
An Only Sister. By Madame DE WITT.
Spinning Wheel Stories. By Miss ALCOTT.
My Summer in a Garden. By C. DUDLEY WARNER.

*Low's Pocket Encyclopædia: a Compendium of General Know-*
ledge for Ready Reference. Upwards of 25,000 References, with
Plates. New ed., imp. 32mo, cloth, marbled edges, 3*s.* 6*d.*; roan, 4*s.* 6*d.*

*Low's Handbook to London Charities.* Yearly, cloth, 1*s.* 6*d.*;
paper, 1*s.*

*Lusignan (Princess A. de) Twelve years' Reign of Abdul Hamid*
II. Crown 8vo, 7*s.* 6*d.*

*MᶜCULLOCH (H.) Men and Measures of Half a century.*
Sketches and Comments. 8vo, 18*s.*

*Macdonald (D.) Oceania. Linguistic and Anthropological.*
Illust., and Tables. Crown 8vo, 6*s.*

*Mac Donald (George).* See LOW'S STANDARD NOVELS.

*Macgregor (John) "Rob Roy" on the Baltic.* 3rd Edition,
small post 8vo, 2*s.* 6*d.*; cloth, gilt edges, 3*s.* 6*d.*

—— *A Thousand Miles in the "Rob Roy" Canoe.* 11th
Edition, small post 8vo, 2*s.* 6*d.*; cloth, gilt edges, 3*s.* 6*d.*

—— *Voyage Alone in the Yawl "Rob Roy."* New Edition,
with additions, small post 8vo, 3*s.* 6*d.* and 2*s.* 6*d.*

*Mackenzie (Sir Morell) Fatal Illness of Frederick the Noble.*
Crown 8vo, limp cloth, 2*s.* 6*d.*

*Mackenzie (Rev. John) Austral Africa : Losing it or Ruling it ?*
Illustrations and Maps. 2 vols., 8vo, 32*s.*

*Maclean (H. E.) Maid of the Golden Age.* Illust., cr. 8vo, 6*s.*

*McLellan's Own Story : The War for the Union.* Illust. 18*s.*

*Maginn (W.) Miscellanies. Prose and Verse. With Memoir.*
2 vols., crown 8vo, 24*s.*

*Main (Mrs.; Mrs. Fred Burnaby) High Life and Towers of*
Silence. Illustrated, square 8vo, 10*s.* 6*d.*

*Malan (C. F. de M.) Eric and Connie's Cruise in the South*
Pacific. Crown 8vo, 5*s.*

*Manning (E. F.) Delightful Thames.* Illustrated. 4to, fancy
boards, 5*s*.

*Markham (Clements R.) The Fighting Veres, Sir F. and Sir H.*
8vo, 18*s*.

———— *War between Peru and Chili,* 1879-1881. Third Ed.
Crown 8vo, with Maps, 10*s*. 6*d*.

———— See also "Foreign Countries," MAURY, and VERES.

*Marston (W.) Eminent Recent Actors, Reminiscences Critical,*
&c. 2 vols. Crown 8vo, 21*s*.; new edit., 1 vol., 6*s*.

*Martin (J. W.) Float Fishing and Spinning in the Nottingham*
Style. New Edition. Crown 8vo, 2*s*. 6*d*.

*Matthews (J. W., M.D.) Incwadi Yami : Twenty years in*
South Africa. With many Engravings, royal 8vo, 14*s*.

*Maury (Commander) Physical Geography of the Sea, and its*
Meteorology. New Edition, with Charts and Diagrams, cr. 8vo, 6*s*.

———— *Life.* By his Daughter. Edited by Mr. CLEMENTS R.
MARKHAM. With portrait of Maury. 8vo, 12*s*. 6*d*.

*Melio (G. L.) Manual of Swedish Drill for Teachers and*
Students. Cr. 8vo, 1*s*. 6*d*.

*Men of Mark : Portraits of the most Eminent Men of the Day.*
Complete in 7 Vols., 4to, handsomely bound, gilt edges, 25*s*. each.

*Mendelssohn Family (The),* 1729 — 1847. From Letters and
Journals. Translated. New Edition, 2 vols., 8vo, 30*s*.

*Mendelssohn.* See also " Great Musicians."

*Merrifield's Nautical Astronomy.* Crown 8vo, 7*s*. 6*d*.

*Mills (J.) Alternative Elementary Chemistry.* Ill., cr.8vo, 1*s*.6*d*.

*Mitford (Mary Russell) Our Village.* With 12 full-page and 157
smaller Cuts. Cr. 4to, cloth, gilt edges, 21*s*.; cheaper binding, 10*s*.6*d*.

*Mody (Mrs.) Outlines of German Literature.* 18mo, 1*s*.

*Moffatt (W.) Land and Work ; Depression, Agricultural and*
Commercial. Crown 8vo, 5*s*.

*Mohammed Benani : A Story of To-day.* 8vo, 10*s*. 6*d*.

*Mollett (J. W.) Illustrated Dictionary of Words used in Art and*
Archæology. Illustrated, small 4to, 15*s*.

*Moore (J. M.) New Zealand for Emigant, Invalid and Tourist.*
Cr. 8vo.

*Morley (Henry) English Literature in the Reign of Victoria.*
2000th volume of the Tauchnitz Collection of Authors. 18mo, 2*s*. 6*d*.

*Mormonism.* See STENHOUSE.

*Morse (E. S.) Japanese Homes and their Surroundings.* With
more than 300 Illustrations. Re-issue, 10*s*. 6*d*.

*Morten (Honnor) Sketches of Hospital Life.* Cr. 8vo, sewed, 1*s*.

*Morwood. Our Gipsies in City, Tent, and Van.* 8vo, 18*s*.

*Moss (F. J.) Through Atolls and Islands of the great South Sea.*
Illust., crown 8vo, 8*s*.`6*d*.

*Moxon (Walter) Pilocereus Senilis.* Fcap. 8vo, gilt top, 3s. 6d.
*Muller (E.) Noble Words and Noble Deeds.* Illustrated, gilt
    edges, 3s. 6d.; plainer binding, 2s. 6d.
*Musgrave (Mrs.) Miriam.* Crown 8vo, 6s.
*Music.* See "Great Musicians."

*NETHERCOTE (C. B.) Pytchley Hunt.* New Ed., cr. 8vo,
    8s. 6d.
*New Zealand.* See BRADSHAW and WHITE (J.).
*New Zealand Rulers and Statesmen.* See GISBORNE.
*Nicholls (J. H. Kerry) The King Country: Explorations in*
    New Zealand. Many Illustrations and Map. New Edition, 8vo, 21s.
*Nordhoff (C.) California, for Health, Pleasure, and Residence.*
    New Edition, 8vo, with Maps and Illustrations, 12s. 6d.
*Norman (C. B.) Corsairs of France.* With Portraits. 8vo, 18s.
*North (W.; M.A.) Roman Fever: an Inquiry during three*
    years' residence. Illust., 8vo, 25s.
*Northbrook Gallery.* Edited by LORD RONALD GOWER. 36 Per-
    manent Photographs. Imperial 4to, 63s.; large paper, 105s.
*Nott (Major) Wild Animals Photographed and Described.* 35s.
*Nursery Playmates (Prince of).* 217 Coloured Pictures for
    Children by eminent Artists. Folio, in col. bds., 6s.; new ed., 2s. 6d.
*Nursing Record.* Yearly, 8s.; half-yearly, 4s. 6d.; quarterly,
    2s. 6d; weekly, 2d.

*O'BRIEN (R. B.) Fifty Years of Concessions to Ireland.*
    With a Portrait of T. Drummond. Vol. I., 16s., II., 16s.
*Orient Line Guide.* New edition re-written; by W. J. LOFTIE.
    Maps and Plans, 2s. 6d.
*Orvis (C. F.) Fishing with the Fly.* Illustrated. 8vo, 12s. 6d.
*Osborne (Duffield) Spell of Ashtaroth.* Crown 8vo, 5s.
*Our Little Ones in Heaven.* Edited by the Rev. H. ROBBINS.
    With Frontispiece after Sir JOSHUA REYNOLDS. New Edition, 5s.

*PALGRAVE (R. F. D.) Oliver Cromwell and his Protec-*
    torate. Crown 8vo.
*Pall ser (M. s.) A History of Lace.* New Edition, with addi-
    tional cuts and text. 8vo, 21s.
—— *The China Collector's Pocket Companion.* With up-
    wards of 1000 Illustrations of Marks and Monograms. Small 8vo, 5s.
*Panton (J. E.) Homes of Taste. Hints on Furniture and Deco-*
    ration. Crown 8vo, 2s. 6d.
*Parsons (James; A.M.) Exposition of the Principles of Partner-*
    ship. 8vo, 31s. 6d.

*Pennell (H. Cholmondeley) Sporting Fish of Great Britain*
15s. ; large paper, 30s.
—— *Modern Improvements in Fishing-tackle.* Crown 8vo, 2s.
*Perelaer (M. T. H.) Ran Au ay from the Dutch ; Borneo, &c.*
Illustrated, square 8vo, 7s. 6d ; new ed., 2s. 6d.
*Perry (J. J. M.) Edlingham Burglary, or Circumstantial Evi-*
dence. Crown 8vo, 3s. 6d.
*Phelps (Elizabeth Stuart) Struggle for Immortality.* Cr. 8vo, 5s.
*Phillips' Dictionary of Biographical Reference.* New edition,
royal 8vo, 25s.
*Philpot (II. J.) Diabc es Melli us.* Crown 8vo, 5s.
—— *Diet System.* Tables. I. Diabetes; II. Gout;
III. Dyspepsia ; IV. Corpulence. In cases, 1s. each.
*Plunkett (Major G. T.) Primer of Orthographic Projection.*
Elementary Solid Geometry. With Problems and Exercises. 2s. 6d.
*Poe (E. A.) The Raven.* Illustr. by DORÉ. Imperial folio, 63s.
*Poems of the Inner Life.* Chiefly Modern. Small 8vo, 5s.
*Poetry of the Anti-Jacobin.* New ed., by CHARLES EDMONDS.
Cr. 8vo, 7s. 6d.; large paper, 21s.
*Porcher (A.) Juven le French Plays.* With Notes and a
Vocabulary. 18mo, 1s.
*Porter (Admiral David D.) Naval History of Civil War.*
Portraits, Plans, &c. 4to, 25s.
*Portraits of Celebrated Race-horses of the Past and Present*
Centuries. with Pedigrees and Performances. 4 vols., 4to, 126s.
*Powles (L. D.) Land of the Pink Pearl : Life in the Bahamas.*
8vo, 10s. 6d.
*Poynter (Edward J., R.A.).* See " Illustrated Text-books."
*Prince Maskiloff : a Romance of Modern Oxford.* By ROY
TELLET. Crown 8vo, 10s. 6d.
*Prince of Nursery Playmates.* Col. plates, new ed., 2s. 6d.
*Pritt (T. E.) North Country Flies.* Illustrated from the
Author's Drawings. 10s. 6d.
*Publishers' Circular (The), and General Record of British and*
Foreign Literature. Published on the 1st and 15th of every Month, 3d.
*Pyle (Howard) Otto of the Silver Hand.* Illustrated by the
Author. 8vo, 8s. 6d.


*QUEEN'S Prime Ministers.* A series. Edited by S. J. REID.
Cr. 8vo, 2s. 6d. per vol.


*RAMBAUD. History of Russia.* New Edition, Illustrated.
3 vols., 8vo, 21s.

*Reber. History of Mediæval Art.* Translated by CLARKE.
422 Illustrations and Glossary. 8vo,    .

*Redford (G.) Ancient Sculpture.* New Ed. Crown 8vo, 10s. 6d.

*Redgrave (G. R.) Century of Painters of the English School.*
Crown 8vo, 10s. 6d.

*Reed (Sir E. J., M.P.) and Simpson. Modern Ships of War.*
Illust., royal 8vo, 10s. 6d.

*Reed (Talbot B.) Sir Ludar : a Tale of the Days of good Queen*
Bess. Crown 8vo, 6s.

*Remarkable Bindings in the British Museum.* India paper,
94s. 6d. ; sewed 73s. 6d. and 63s.

*Reminiscences of a Boyhood in the early part of the Century : a*
Story. Crown 8vo, 6s.

*Ricci (J. H. de) Fisheries Dispute, and the Annexation of*
Canada. Crown 8vo, 6s.

*Richards (W.) Aluminium: its History, Occurrence, &c.*
Illustrated, crown 8vo, 12s. 6d.

*Richter (Dr. Jean Paul) Italian Art in the National Gallery.*
4to. Illustrated. Cloth gilt, £2 2s.; half-morocco, uncut, £2 12s. 6d.

—— See also LEONARDO DA VINCI.

*Riddell (Mrs. J. H.)* See LOW'S STANDARD NOVELS.

*Roberts (W.) Earlier History of English Bookselling.* Crown
8vo, 7s. 6d.

*Robertson (T. W.) Principal Dramatic Works, with Portraits*
in photogravure. 2 vols., 21s.

*Robin Hood; Merry Adventures of.* Written and illustrated
by HOWARD PYLE. Imperial 8vo, 15s.

*Robinson (Phil.) In my Indian Garden.* New Edition, 16mo,
limp cloth, 2s.

—— *Noah's Ark. Unnatural History.* Sm. post 8vo, 12s. 6d.

—— *Sinners and Saints : a Tour across the United States of*
America, and Round them. Crown 8vo, 10s. 6d.

—— *Under the Punkah.* New Ed , cr. 8vo, limp cloth, 2s.

*Rockstro (W. S.) History of Music.* New Edition. 8vo, 14s.

*Roe (E. P.) Nature's Serial Story.* Illust. New ed. 3s. 6d.

*Roland, The Story of.* Crown 8vo, illustrated, 6s.

*Rose (J.) Complete Practical Machinist.* New Ed., 12mo, 12s. 6d.

—— *Key to Engines and Engine-running.* Crown 8vo, 8s. 6d.

—— *Mechanical Drawing.* Illustrated, small 4to, 16s.

—— *Modern Steam Engines.* Illustrated. 31s. 6d.

—— *Steam Boilers. Boiler Construction and Examination.*
Illust., 8vo, 12s. 6d.

*Rose Library.* Each volume, 1*s.* Many are illustrated—
**Little Women.** By LOUISA M. ALCOTT.
**Little Women Wedded.** Forming a Sequel to "Little Women.
**Little Women and Little Women Wedded.** 1 vol., cloth gilt, 3*s.* 6*d.*
**Little Men.** By L. M. ALCOTT. Double vol., 2*s.*; cloth gilt, 3*s.* 6*d.*
**An Old-Fashioned Girl.** By LOUISA M. ALCOTT. 2*s.*; cloth, 3*s.* 6*d.*
**Work.** A Story of Experience. By L. M. ALCOTT. 3*s.* 6*d.*; 2 vols., 1*s.* each.
**Stowe (Mrs. H. B.) The Pearl of Orr's Island.**
———— **The Minister's Wooing.**
———— **We and our Neighbours.** 2*s.*; cloth gilt, 6*s.*
———— **My Wife and I.** 2*s.*
**Hans Brinker; or, the Silver Skates.** By Mrs. DODGE. Also 2*s.*6*d.*
**My Study Windows.** By J. R. LOWELL.
**The Guardian Angel.** By OLIVER WENDELL HOLMES. Cloth, 2*s.*
**My Summer in a Garden.** By C. D. WARNER.
**Dred.** By Mrs. BEECHER STOWE. 2*s.*; cloth gilt, 3*s.* 6*d.*
**City Ballads.** New Ed. 16mo. By WILL CARLETON.
**Farm Ballads.** By WILL CARLETON. ⎫
**Farm Festivals.** By WILL CARLETON. ⎬ 1 vol., cl., gilt ed., 3*s.* 6*d.*
**Farm Legends.** By WILL CARLETON. ⎭
**The Rose in Bloom.** By L. M. ALCOTT. 2*s.*; cloth gilt, 3*s.* 6*d.*
**Eight Cousins.** By L. M. ALCOTT. 2*s.*; cloth gilt, 3*s.* 6*d.*
**Under the Lilacs.** By L. M. ALCOTT. 2*s.*; also 3*s.* 6*d.*
**Undiscovered Country.** By W. D. HOWELLS.
**Clients of Dr. Bernagius.** By L. BIART. 2 parts.
**Silver Pitchers.** By LOUISA M. ALCOTT. Cloth, 3*s.* 6*d.*
**Jimmy's Cruise in the "Pinafore," and other Tales.** By LOUISA M. ALCOTT. 2*s.*; cloth gilt, 3*s.* 6*d.*
**Jack and Jill.** By LOUISA M. ALCOTT. 2*s.*; Illustrated, 5*s.*
**Hitherto.** By the Author of the "Gayworthys." 2 vols., 1*s.* each; 1 vol., cloth gilt, 3*s.* 6*d.*
**A Gentleman of Leisure.** A Novel. By EDGAR FAWCETT. 1*s.*

See also LOW'S STANDARD SERIES.

*Ross (Mars) and Stonehewer Cooper. Highlands of Cantabria;* or, Three Days from England. Illustrations and Map, 8vo, 21*s.*
*Rothschilds, the Financial Rulers of Nations.* By JOHN REEVES. Crown 8vo, 7*s.* 6*d.*
*Rousselet (Louis) Son of the Constable of France.* Small post 8vo, numerous Illustrations, gilt edges, 3*s.* 6*d.*; plainer, 2*s.* 6*d.*
———— *King of the Tigers: a Story of Central India.* Illustrated. Small post 8vo, gilt, 3*s.* 6*d.*; plainer, 2*s.* 6*d.*
———— *Drummer Boy.* Illustrated. Small post 8vo, gilt edges, 3*s.* 6*d.*; plainer, 2*s.* 6*d.*
*Russell (Dora) Strange Message.* 3 vols., crown 8vo, 31*s.* 6*d.*
*Russell (W. Clark) Betwixt the Forelands.* Illust., crown 8vo, 10*s.* 6*d.*

*Russell (W. Clark) English Channel Ports and the Estate* of the East and West India Dock Company. Crown 8vo, 1s.

———— *Sailor's Language.* Illustrated. Crown 8vo, 3s. 6d.

———— *Wreck of the Grosvenor.* 4to, sewed, 6d.

———— See also " Low's Standard Novels," " Sea Stories."

*SAINTS and their Symbols: A Companion in the Churches* and Picture Galleries of Europe. Illustrated. Royal 16mo, 3s. 6d.

*Samuels (Capt. J. S.) From Forecastle to Cabin: Autobiography.* Illustrated. Crown 8vo, 8s. 6d.; also with fewer Illustrations, cloth, 2s.; paper, 1s.

*Saunders (A.) Our Domestic Birds: Poultry in England and* New Zealand. Crown 8vo, 6s.

———— *Our Horses: the Best Muscles controlled by the Best* Brains. 6s.

*Scherr (Prof. J.) History of English Literature.* Cr. 8vo, 8s. 6d.

*Schuyler (Eugène) American Diplomacy and the Furtherance of* Commerce. 12s. 6d.

———— *The Life of Peter the Great.* 2 vols., 8vo, 32s.

*Schweinfurth (Georg) Heart of Africa.* 2 vols., crown 8vo, 15s.

*Scott (Leader) Renaissance of Art in Italy.* 4to, 31s. 6d.

———— *Sculpture, Renaissance and Modern.* 5s.

*Sea Stories.* By W. CLARK RUSSELL. New ed. Cr. 8vo, leather back, top edge gilt, per vol., 3s. 6d.

| | |
|---|---|
| Frozen Pirate. | Sea Queen. |
| Jack's Courtship. | Strange Voyage. |
| John Holdsworth. | The Lady Maud. |
| Little Loo. | Watch Below. |
| Ocean Free Lance. | Wreck of the *Grosvenor*. |
| Sailor's Sweetheart. | |

*Semmes (Adm. Raphael) Service Afloat: The " Sumter " and* the " Alabama." Illustrated. Royal 8vo, 16s.

*Senior (W.) Near and Far: an Angler's Sketches of Home* Sport and Colonial Life. Crown 8vo, 6s.; new edit., 2s.

———— *Waterside Sketches.* Imp. 32mo, 1s. 6d.; boards, 1s.

*Shakespeare.* Edited by R. GRANT WHITE. 3 vols., crown 8vo, gilt top, 36s.; *Édition de luxe*, 6 vols., 8vo, cloth extra, 63s.

*Shakespeare's Heroines: Studies by Living English Painters.* 105s.; artists' proofs, 630s.

———— *Macbeth.* With Etchings on Copper, by J. MOYR SMITH. 105s. and 52s. 6d.

———— *Songs and Sonnets.* Illust. by Sir JOHN GILBERT, R.A. 4to, boards, 5s.

———— See also CUNDALL, DETHRONING, DONNELLY, MACKAY, and WHITE (R. GRANT).

*Sharpe (R. Bowdler) Birds in Nature.* 39 coloured plates
and text. 4to, 63*s.*

*Sheridan. Rivals.* Reproductions of Water-colour, &c. 52*s.6d.;*
artists proofs, 105*s.* nett.

*Shields (C. W.) Philosophia ultima ; from Harmony of Science*
and Religion. 2 vols. 8vo, 24*s.*

*Shields (G. O.) Cruisings in the Cascades; Hunting, Photo-*
graphy, Fishing. 8vo, 10*s. 6d.*

*Sidney (Sir Philip) Arcadia.* New Edition, 3*s. 6d.*

*Siegfried, The Story of.* Illustrated, crown 8vo, cloth, 6*s.*

*Simon. China : its Social Life.* Crown 8vo, 6*s.*

*Simson (A.) Wilds of Ecuador and Exploration of the Putumayor*
River. Crown 8vo, 8*s. 6d.*

*Sinclair (Mrs.) Indigenous Flowers of the Hawaiian Islands.*
44 Plates in Colour. Imp. folio, extra binding, gilt edges, 31*s. 6d.*

*Sloane (T. O.) Home Experiments in Science for Old and Young.*
Crown 8vo, 6*s.*

*Smith (G.) Assyrian Explorations.* Illust. New Ed., 8vo, 18*s*
———— *The Chaldean Account of Genesis.* With many Illustrations. 16*s.* New Ed. By PROFESSOR SAYCE. 8vo, 18*s.*

*Smith (G. Barnett) William I. and the German Empire.*
New Ed., 8vo, 3*s. 6d.*

*Smith (Sydney) Life and Times.* By STUART J. REID. Illustrated. 8vo, 21*s.*

*Spiers' French Dictionary.* 29th Edition, remodelled. 2 vols.,
8vo, 18*s.;* half bound, 21*s.*

*Spry (W. J. J., R.N., F.R.G.S.) Cruise of H.M.S." Challenger."*
With Illustrations. 8vo, 18*s.* Cheap Edit., crown 8vo, 7*s. 6d.*

*Stanley (H. M.) Congo, and Founding its Free State.* Illustrated,
2 vols., 8vo, 42*s.* ; re-issue, 2 vols. 8vo, 21*s*
———— *How I Found Livingstone.* 8vo, 10*s. 6d.* ; cr. 8vo, 7*s. 6d.*
——— *Through the Dark Continent.* Crown 8vo, 12*s. 6d.*

*Start (J. W. K.) Junior Mensuration Exercises.* 8*d.*

*Stenhouse (Mrs.) Tyranny of Mormonism.* An *Englishwoman*
in Utah. New ed., cr. 8vo, cloth elegant, 3*s. 6d.*

*Sterry (J. Ashby) Cucumber Chronicles.* 5*s.*

*Stevens (E. W.) Fly-Fishing in Maine Lakes.* 8*s. 6d.*

*Stevens (T.) Around the World on a Bicycle.* Vol. II. 8vo. 16*s.*

*Stockton (Frank R.) Rudder Grange.* 3*s. 6d.*
———— *Bee-Man of Orn, and other Fanciful Tales.* Cr. 8vo, 5*s.*
———— *Personally conducted.* Crown 8vo, 7*s. 6d.*
———— *The Casting Away of Mrs. Lecks and Mrs. Aleshine.* 1*s.*
——— *The Dusantes.* Sequel to the above. Sewed, 1*s.;*
this and the preceding book in one volume, cloth, 2*s. 6d.*

*Stockton (Frank R.) The Hundredth Man.* Small post 8vo, 6s.
—— *The Late Mrs. Null.* Small post 8vo, 6s.
——— *The Story of Viteau.* Illust. Cr. 8vo, 5s.
——— See also Low's STANDARD NOVELS.
*Stowe (Mrs. Beecher) Dred.* Cloth, gilt edges, 3s. 6d.; cloth, 2s.
—— *Flowers and Fruit from her Writings.* Sm. post 8vo, 3s. 6d.
—— *Life, in her own Words . . . with Letters and Original* Compositions. 10s. 6d.
—— *Little Foxes.* Cheap Ed., 1s.; Library Edition, 4s. 6d.
—— *My Wife and I.* Cloth, 2s.
—— *Old Town Folk.* 6s.
—— *We and our Neighbours.* 2s.
—— *Poganuc People.* 6s.
—— See also ROSE LIBRARY.
*Strachan (J.) Explorations and Adventures in New Guinea.* Illust., crown 8vo, 12s.
*Stranahan (C. H.) History of French Painting, the Academy,* Salons, Schools, &c. 21s.
*Stutfield (Hugh E. M.) El Maghreb:* 1200 *Miles' Ride through* Marocco. 8s. 6d.
*Sullivan (A. M.) Nutshell History of Ireland.* Paper boards, 6d.
*Sylvanus Redivivus, Rev. J. Mitford, with a Memoir of E.* Jesse. Crown 8vo, 10s. 6d.


*TAINE (H. A.) " Origines."* Translated by JOHN DURAND.
    I.  **The Ancient Regime.** Demy 8vo, cloth, 16s.
    II.  **The French Revolution.** Vol. 1.  do.
    III.  **Do.**  do.  Vol. 2.  do.
    IV.  **Do.**  do.  Vol. 3.  do.
*Tauchnitz's English Editions of German Authors.* Each volume, cloth flexible, 2s. ; or sewed, 1s. 6d. (Catalogues post free.)
*Tauchnitz (B.) German Dictionary.* 2s.; paper, 1s. 6d.; roan, 2s. 6d.
—— *French Dictionary.* 2s. ; paper, 1s. 6d. ; roan, 2s. 6d.
—— *Italian Dictionary.* 2s. ; paper, 1s. 6d. ; roan, 2s. 6d.
—— *Latin Dictionary.* 2s.; paper, 1s. 6d. ; roan, 2s. 6d.
—— *Spanish and English.* 2s. ; paper, 1s. 6d. ; roan, 2s. 6d.
—— *Spanish and French.* 2s.; paper, 1s. 6d. ; roan, 2s. 6d.
*Taylor (R. L.) Chemical Analysis Tables.* 1s.
—— *Chemistry for Beginners.* Small 8vo, 1s. 6d.
*Techno-Chemical Receipt Book.* With additions by BRANNT and WAHL. 10s. 6d.

*Technological Dictionary.* See TOLHAUSEN.

*Thausing (Prof.) Malt and the Fabrication of Beer.* 8vo, 45*s.*

*Theakston (M.) British Angling Flies.* Illustrated. Cr. 8vo, 5*s.*

*Thomson (Jos.) Central African Lakes.* New edition, 2 vols. in one, crown 8vo, 7*s.* 6*d.*

———— *Through Masai Land.* Illust. 21*s.*; new edition, 7*s.* 6*d.*

———— *and Miss Harris-Smith. Ulu: an African Romance.* crown 8vo. 6*s.*

*Thomson ( W.) Algebra for Colleges and Schools.* With Answers, 5*s.*; without, 4*s.* 6*d.*; Answers separate, 1*s.* 6*d.*

*Thornton (L. D.) Story of a Poodle.* By Himself and his Mistress. Illust., crown 4to, 2*s.* 6*d.*

*Thorrodsen, Lad and Lass.* Translated from the Icelandic by A. M. REEVES. Crown 8vo.

*Tissandier (G.) Eiffel Tower.* Illust., and letter of M. Eiffel in facsimile. Fcap. 8vo, 1*s.*

*Tolhausen. Technological German, English, and French Dictionary.* Vols. I., II., with Supplement, 12*s.* 6*d.* each; III., 9*s.*; Supplement, cr. 8vo, 3*s.* 6*d.*

*Topmkins (E. S. de G.) Through David's Realm.* Illust. by the Author. 8vo, 10*s.* 6*d.*

*Tucker ( W. J.) Life and Society in Eastern Europe.* 15*s.*

*Tuckerman (B.) Life of General Lafayette.* 2 vols., cr. 8vo, 12*s.*

*Tupper (Martin Farquhar) My Life as an Author.* 14*s.*; new edition, 7*s.* 6*d.*

*Tytler (Sarah) Duchess Frances: a Novel.* 2 vols., 21*s.*


*UPTON (H.) Manual of Practical Dairy Farming.* Cr. 8vo, 2*s.*


*VAN DAM. Land of Rubens; a companion for visitors to* Belgium. Crown 8vo, 3*s.* 6*d.*

*Vane ( Young Sir Harry).* By Prof. JAMES K. HOSMER. 8vo, 18*s.*

*Veres. Biography of Sir Francis Vere and Lord Vere, leading* Generals in the Netherlands. By CLEMENTS R. MARKHAM. 8vo, 18*s.*

*Verne (Jules) Celebrated Travels and Travellers.* 3 vols. 8vo, 7*s.* 6*d.* each; extra gilt, 9*s.*

*Victoria (Queen) Life of.* By GRACE GREENWOOD. Illust. 6*s.*

*Vincent (Mrs. Howard) Forty Thousand Miles over Land and* Water. With Illustrations. New Edit., 3*s.* 6*d.*

*Viollet-le-Duc (E.) Lectures on Architecture.* Translated by BENJAMIN BUCKNALL, Architect. 2 vols., super-royal 8vo, £3 3*s.*

# BOOKS BY JULES VERNE.

| LARGE CROWN 8vo. | Containing 350 to 600 pp. and from 50 to 100 full-page illustrations. | | Containing the whole o text with some illustra |
|---|---|---|---|
| **WORKS.** | In very handsome cloth binding, gilt edges. | In plainer binding, plain edges. | In cloth binding, gilt edges, smaller type. | Coloured b or clot |

| WORKS. | In very handsome cloth binding, gilt edges. | In plainer binding, plain edges. | In cloth binding, gilt edges, smaller type. | Coloured b or clot |
|---|---|---|---|---|
| | s. d. | s. d. | s. d. | |
| 20,000 Leagues under the Sea. Parts I. and II. | 10 6 | 5 0 | 3 6 | 2 vols., 1s. |
| Hector Servadac | 10 6 | 5 0 | 3 6 | 2 vols., 1s. |
| The Fur Country | 10 6 | 5 0 | 3 0 | 2 vols., 1s. |
| The Earth to the Moon and a Trip round it | 10 6 | 5 0 | { 2 vols., 2s. ea. } | 2 vols., 1s. |
| Michael Strogoff | 10 6 | 5 0 | 3 6 | 2 vols., 1s. |
| Dick Sands, the Boy Captain | 10 6 | 5 0 | 3 6 | 2 vols., 1s. |
| Five Weeks in a Balloon | 7 6 | 3 6 | 2 0 | 1s. 0 |
| Adventures of Three Englishmen and Three Russians | 7 6 | 3 6 | 2 0 | 1 0 |
| Round the World in Eighty Days | 7 6 | 3 6 | 2 0 | 1 0 |
| A Floating City | 7 6 | 3 6 | { 2 0 | 1 0 |
| The Blockade Runners | | | 2 0 | 1 0 |
| Dr. Ox's Experiment | — | — | 2 0 | 1 0 |
| A Winter amid the Ice | — | — | 2 0 | 1 0 |
| Survivors of the "Chancellor" | 7 6 | 3 6 | { 3 6 | 2 vols., 1s. |
| Martin Paz | | | 2 0 | 1s. 0 |
| The Mysterious Island, 3 vols. :— | 22 6 | 10 6 | 6 0 | 3 0 |
| I. Dropped from the Clouds | 7 6 | 3 6 | 2 0 | 1 0 |
| II. Abandoned | 7 6 | 3 6 | 2 0 | 1 0 |
| III. Secret of the Island | 7 6 | 3 6 | 2 0 | 1 0 |
| The Child of the Cavern | 7 6 | 3 6 | 2 0 | 1 0 |
| The Begum's Fortune | 7 6 | 3 6 | 2 0 | 1 0 |
| The Tribulations of a Chinaman | 7 6 | 3 6 | 2 0 | 1 0 |
| The Steam House, 2 vols. :— | | | | |
| I. Demon of Cawnpore | 7 6 | 3 6 | 2 0 | 1 0 |
| II. Tigers and Traitors | 7 6 | 3 6 | 2 0 | 1 0 |
| The Giant Raft, 2 vols. :— | | | | |
| I. 800 Leagues on the Amazon | 7 6 | 3 6 | 2 0 | 1 0 |
| II. The Cryptogram | 7 6 | 3 6 | 2 0 | 1 0 |
| The Green Ray | 6 0 | 5 0 | — | 1 0 |
| Godfrey Morgan | 7 6 | 3 6 | 2 0 | 1 0 |
| Kéraban the Inflexible:— | | | | |
| I. Captain of the "Guidara" | 7 6 | 3 6 | 2 0 | 1 0 |
| II. Scarpante the Spy | 7 6 | 3 6 | 2 0 | 1 0 |
| The Archipelago on Fire | 7 6 | 3 6 | 2 0 | 1 0 |
| The Vanished Diamond | 7 6 | 3 6 | 2 0 | 1 0 |
| Mathias Sandorf | 10 6 | 5 0 | 3 6 | 2 vols., 1s |
| The Lottery Ticket | 7 6 | 3 6 | | |
| The Clipper of the Clouds | 7 6 | 3 6 | | |
| North against South | 7 6 | | | |
| Adrift in the Pacific | 7 6 | | | |
| Flight to France | 7 6 | | | |

CELEBRATED TRAVELS AND TRAVELLERS. 3 vols. 8vo, 600 pp., 100 full-page illustrations, gilt edges, 14s. each :—(1) THE EXPLORATION OF THE WORLD. (2) THE GREAT NAVIGATORS EIGHTEENTH CENTURY. (3) THE GREAT EXPLORERS OF THE NINETEENTH CENTURY.

*WALFORD (Mrs. L. B.) Her Great Idea, and other Stories.* Cr. 8vo, 10s. 6d.; also new ed., 6s.

*Wallace (L.) Ben Hur: A Tale of the Christ.* New Edition, crown 8vo, 6s.; cheaper edition, 2s.

*Wallack (L.) Memories of 50 Years; with many Portraits, and* Facsimiles. Small 4to, 63s. nett; ordinary edition 7s. 6d.

*Waller(Rev. C.H.) Adoption and the Covenant.* On Confirmation. 2s. 6d.

—— *Silver Sockets; and other Shadows of Redemption.* Sermons at Christ Church, Hampstead. Small post 8vo, 6s.

—— *The Names on the Gates of Pearl, and other Studies.* New Edition. Crown 8vo, cloth extra, 3s. 6d.

—— *Words in the Greek Testament.* Part I. Grammar. Small post 8vo, cloth, 2s. 6d. Part II. Vocabulary, 2s. 6d.

*Walsh(A. S.) Mary, Queen of the House of David.* 8vo, 3s. 6d.

*Walton (Iz.) Wallet Book,* CIↃIↃLXXXV. Crown 8vo, half vellum, 21s.; large paper, 42s.

—— *Compleat Angler.* Lea and Dove Edition. Ed. by R. B. MARSTON. With full-page Photogravures on India paper, and the Woodcuts on India paper from blocks. 4to, half-morocco, 105s.; large paper, royal 4to, full dark green morocco, gilt top, 210s.

*Walton (T. H.) Coal Mining.* With Illustrations. 4to, 25s.

*War Scare in Europe.* Crown 8vo, 2s. 6d.

*Warner (C. D.) My Summer in a Garden.* Boards, 1s.; leatherette, 1s. 6d.; cloth, 2s.

—— *Their Pilgrimage.* Illustrated by C. S. REINHART. 8vo, 7s. 6d.

*Warren (W. F.) Paradise Found; the North Pole the Cradle* of the Human Race. Illustrated. Crown 8vo, 12s. 6d.

*Washington Irving's Little Britain.* Square crown 8vo, 6s.

*Watson (P. B.) Swedish Revolution under Gustavus Vasa.* 8vo.

*Wells (H. P.) American Salmon Fisherman.* 6s.

—— *Fly Rods and Fly Tackle.* Illustrated. 10s. 6d.

*Wells (J. W.) Three Thousand Miles through Brazil.* Illustrated from Original Sketches. 2 vols. 8vo, 32s.

*Wenzel (O.) Directory of Chemical Products of the German* Empire 8vo, 25s.

*Westgarth (W.) Half-century of Australasian Progress. Personal* retrospect. 8vo, 12s.

*Wheatley (H. B.) Remarkable Bindings in the British Museum.* Reproductions in Colour, 94s. 6d., 73s. 6d., and 63s.

*White (J.) Ancient History of the Maori; Mythology, &c.* Vols. I.-IV. 8vo, 10s. 6d. each.

*White (R. Grant) England Without and Within.* Crown 8vo, 10s. 6d.

—— *Every-day English.* 10s. 6d.

*White* (*R. Grant*) *Fate of Mansfield Humphreys,&c.*   C *l.* 8vo, 6*s.*
———— *Studies in Shakespeare.*   10*s.* 6*d.*
———— *Words and their Uses.*   New Edit., crown 8vo, 5*s.*
*Whitney* (*Mrs.*) *The Other Girls.*   A Sequel to "We Girls."
◢ New ed.   12mo, 2*s.*
———— *We Girls.*   New Edition.   2*s.*
*Whittier* (*J. G.*) *The King's Missive, and later Poems.*   18mo,
choice parchment cover, 3*s.* 6*d.*
———— *St. Gregory's Guest, &c.*   Recent Poems.   5*s.*
*William I. and the German Empire.*   By G. BARNETT SMITH.
New Edition, 3*s.* 6*d.*
*Willis-Bund* (*J.*) *Salmon Problems.*   3*s.* 6*d.*; boards, 2*s.* 6*d.*
*Wills* (*Dr. C. J.*) *Persia as it is.*   Crown 8vo, 8*s.* 6*d.*
*Wills, A Few Hints on Proving, without Professional Assistance.*
By a PROBATE COURT OFFICIAL.   8th Edition, revised, with Forms
of Wills, Residuary Accounts, &c.   Fcap. 8vo, cloth limp, 1*s.*
*Wilmot* (*A.*) *Poetry of South Africa Collected.*   8vo, 6*s.*
*Wilmot-Buxton* (*Ethel M.*) *Wee Folk, Good Folk : a Fantasy.*
Illust., fcap. 4to, 5*s.*
*Winder* (*Frederick Horatio*) *Lost in Africa : a Yarn of Adven-*
ture.   Illust., cr. 8vo, 6*s.*
*Winsor* (*Justin*) *Narrative and Critical History of America.*
8 vols., 30*s.* each ; large paper, per vol., 63*s.*
*Woolsey.   Introduction to International Law.*   5th Ed., 18*s.*)
*Woolson* (*Constance F.*)   See "Low's Standard Novels."
*Wright* (*H.*) *Friendship of God.*   Portrait, &c.   Crown 8vo, 6*s.*
*Wright* (*T.*) *Town of Cowper, Olney, &c.*   6*s.*
*Wrigley* (*M.*) *Algiers Illustrated.*   100 Views in Photogravure.
Royal 4to, 45*s.*
*Written to Order ; the Journeyings of an Irresponsible Egotist.*
By the Author of "A Day of my Life at Eton."   Crown 8vo, 6*s.*

*Y RIARTE* (*Charles*) *Florence : its History.*   Translated by
C. B. PITMAN.   Illustrated with 500 Engravings.   Large imperial
4to, extra binding, gilt edges, 63*s.* ; or 12 Parts, 5*s.* each.

*Z ILLMAN* (*J. H. L.*) *Past and Present Australian Life.*
With Stories.   Crown 8vo, 2*s.*

---

Lonĕon:

SAMPSON LOW, MARSTON, SEARLE, & RIVINGTON, LD.,
St. Đunstan's Đonse,
FETTER LANE, FLEET STREET, E.C.

---

Gilbert and Rivington, Ld., St. John's House, Clerkenwell Road, E.C.